ALSO BY
DARCY COATES

The
HAUNTING
of
GILLESPIE
HOUSE

DARCY COATES

Poisoned Pen
PRESS

Published by Poisoned Pen Press, an imprint of Sourcebooks
P.O. Box 4410, Naperville, Illinois 60567-4410
(630) 961-3900
sourcebooks.com

The Haunting of Gillespie House was originally self-published in 2015 by Black
Owl Books. "Crawlspace" and "Lights Out" were originally self-published in the
short-story collection *Quarter to Midnight* in 2015 by Black Owl Books.

Library of Congress Cataloging-in-Publication Data

Names: Coates, Darcy, author.
Title: Haunting of Gillespie House / Darcy Coates.
Description: Naperville, IL : Poisoned Pen Press, [2020]
Identifiers: LCCN 2019059651 | (trade paperback)
Subjects: LCSH: Paranormal fiction. | GSAFD: Horror fiction. | Occult
    fiction.
Classification: LCC PR9619.4.C628 H4 2020 | DDC 823/.92--dc23
LC record available at https://lccn.loc.gov/2019059651

Printed and bound in the United States of America.
VP 10 9 8 7 6 5 4 3 2 1

CONTENTS

The
HAUNTING
of
GILLESPIE
HOUSE

CHAPTER 1
WHISPERS

THE NIGHT WAS COLD and still. The curtains were too thin to block out the moonlight, which stretched over the carpet in quivering dabs and strange shapes from where it managed to worm its way through the forest's boughs.

A sliver of the light fell over the sleeping girl's face, making her squirm to avoid it. She rolled over and opened her eyes. The dolls and stuffed animals spread around the room watched her with plastic eyes, their comforting influence dissipated in the cold blue light of nighttime.

The girl sat up and pushed her hair out of her face. She thought she'd heard the voices through her dreams; they were becoming clearer, though, almost clear enough to understand.

"Hello?" She kept her voice quiet so she wouldn't disturb her parents as they slept in their room down the hallway. "Is that you, little friends?"

There, so faint that she almost could have imagined it, was the soft scratching noise that accompanied the voice. The girl slid her feet off the bed, shivering in the cold air but too entranced to search for her dressing gown. Her toes dug into the carpet as she circled her bed, trying to find the source of the noise. It seemed to come from all around her, below her feet and above her head. The curtains fluttered as the wind picked up, and the old house groaned under the weight of its years.

"Hello, little friends?" she repeated.

The voices answered her, urging her to come to them. She closed her eyes and stretched out her hands, rotating in a slow circle, listening to the sounds. They seemed to fade and strengthen, depending on the direction she faced. She stopped turning when they were at their loudest and took a hesitant step forward. The voices rose in volume and urgency as she moved closer, and the girl could feel her fingers shaking as she reached for her invisible companions.

They had never been so clear before. The voices were slowly merging, their echoes and mutters colliding into a single voice. As the girl's fingers tapped against her bedroom wall, she finally understood them.

"Yes," she said, breathless, her heart fluttering like a frantic trapped bird. "Yes, I'll help you, little friends."

CHAPTER 2
FIRST DAY

I WAVED AT THE Gillespies' car as it crawled down their driveway, weaving between thickets of trees, then started its journey to the couples' retreat two states away.

Their house stood at my back. It was an old mansion, three stories tall and built mostly of sandstone blocks. The porch had been beautiful once, but the hardwood boards below my sneakers had lost their shine and were developing cracks, and the white paint on the doorway pillars was peeling.

The Gillespies had entrusted the house to my care for the month while they "built on their foundation," as Mrs. Gillespie had put it. But judging by the way the couple actively avoided touching each other, I suspected the foundation had washed away years ago and the retreat was a final effort to keep their marriage from being submerged entirely.

Their house seemed to echo that sentiment. It was a magnificent building—way beyond what I could ever hope to afford with my part-time retail job and useless English degree—but the years hadn't done it any favors. The floorboards creaked under my feet as I passed the threshold and looked around the living room. It was clean, at least, but the furniture had a shabby past-its-prime look, and the off-white walls were edging toward a dingy gray.

I dropped the house key on the coffee table as I passed it, along with a slip of paper with Mrs. Gillespie's cell phone number printed in a neat, feminine script. Beyond the living room was the dining room. A twelve-seater dark-wood table took pride of place below an actual chandelier.

"Wow." I gazed at the crystal beauty as it sparkled in the dim light, hinting at a history of glamorous dinner parties and decadent lifestyles.

I ran my hand through my messy hair, trying to pull out some of the knots. I hadn't washed it the night before, and it felt greasy between my fingers. *Settle in first, shower later.*

Mrs. Gillespie had told me my room was the last door on the left at the end of the second-floor hallway, so I grabbed my travel case and pulled it up the curved stairway. The hallway stretched the length of the house, with four doors on each side, and I was winded by the time I pushed open the last door. I found myself in a neat room with a large window overlooking the woods behind the property.

My suitcase was heavy, loaded with clothes, books, and my laptop, and I heaved it onto the bed to unpack. There might not have been a chandelier in my room, but it did have sconces set into the wall and patterned wallpaper that looked as though it belonged in the 1920s. For all I knew, that might have been when the house was last renovated.

As I hung my T-shirts and jeans in the dark-wood dresser, I couldn't stop marveling at how clean it was. The room had a stuffy feeling that had made me assume every surface would be covered with dust and cobwebs, but Mrs. Gillespie must have been thorough in her sprucing. Despite this, it felt closed in and musty, and as soon as I'd finished hanging up the clothes, I unlocked and opened the windows to let in fresh air.

A slope, spotted with clumps of rocks and spindly weeds, ran down behind the building to meet the pine woods fifty meters away. The trees had to be old; some of them looked so large I would have had no chance of touching my hands if I tried to embrace them. Their tips stretched above my window, possibly even above the roof of the house, and patchy bushes and vines filled in the spaces around their trunks.

I leaned on the windowsill, closing my eyes and inhaling deeply to savor the smell. The air felt so much clearer and crisper here, away from the smog of the city, and I began to pick up faint animal noises from the woods.

A shiver ran down my spine and I grinned to myself. As much as the Gillespies needed their couples' retreat, I thought I might have needed the housesitting job even more. I hadn't fully settled in, and already I felt lighter, as though the stress from the last eight months of studying and working was loosening its hold.

I twirled away from the window and ran back to my travel

case, suddenly eager to finish unpacking and explore the house. I kicked my spare shoes under the bed, left the toiletries on my bedside table for when I found the bathroom, then unceremoniously dumped the laptop and books onto the desk standing opposite the bed.

"Good enough." I grinned and shoved the travel case inside the wardrobe, then left my room, itching to see the rest of the house. I tried the first door down the hallway, but to my disappointment, it was locked.

Maybe Mrs. Gillespie didn't want me getting nosy and only gave me access to some parts of the house. The thought was like a bucket of cold water dropped over me; I loved old buildings, and part of the thrill of the trip had been the opportunity to explore and enjoy the sprawling Gothic mansion. Not actually seeing much of it would have been devastating.

I tried the next door down the hallway, expecting it to also be locked, but I was thrilled when it opened without protest. Beyond the door was another bedroom, smaller than and not quite as clean as mine. I grinned to myself as I looked through it. Unlike my room with its patterned white-and-gray walls and pale-blue bedspread, this new room was decorated all in shades of maroon. Golden leafy designs adorned the wallpaper, which was peeling in many places, exposing a darker wallpaper behind it. The bedspread looked decades old and held a stack of limp blood-red pillows.

"Gorgeous," I murmured to myself, then darted back into the hallway to look into the next room. It was the same size as the last, but had no furniture at all—just a rug rolled into a coil in the corner and a broom leaning against the wall.

The door opposite that room opened into a bathroom that was old-fashioned but large, with a claw-foot tub. A wide mirror hung above the sink, and the relatively modern shower had probably been installed within the last decade.

The final room was clearly the master bedroom, probably where the Gillespies slept. The queen-size bed had been hastily made, and the wardrobe doors stood open, showing it was still half-full. *Guess I'm not the only one who packs in a hurry.* I didn't want to snoop around their personal things too much, so I left the room without touching anything.

The end of the hallway split into two: to the right was the staircase to the ground floor, and to the left was a staircase going up to the third level. I hesitated, savoring the possibilities of what the top floor might hold, but I knew it made more sense to familiarize myself with the functional parts of the house first. I reluctantly took the stairs down, vowing to explore the upstairs rooms to my heart's content after I'd showered and sorted out dinner.

The lowest level had a strange arrangement, with doors in odd places and clashing aesthetics. I went from the living room to the dining room, then into the kitchen, which was disconcertingly modern compared to the rest of the house. A magnet held a piece of paper to the fridge's silver door: "Please help yourself." I opened the doors and found bacon, vegetables, eggs, milk, and a packet of meat. At least I wasn't going to starve before I could get to the shops in the town half an hour away.

I hadn't realized how remote the Gillespies' house was until I'd arrived. I'd caught a taxi from the train station in the town, and by the time we'd driven past farmland, uphill through the narrow, winding roads hedged on both sides by woods, and eventually pulled up at the brooding stone building, the fare had grown to nearly twice what I'd expected. That meant I didn't have the budget to go into town as often as I'd planned, and I would have to do my shopping in large, infrequent batches.

Not that I minded too much, though. I found the isolation exhilarating. I felt as though I could do anything—*anything!*—and no one would know or care. There was no cranky Mrs. Bobinsky upstairs to complain to the landlord if I watched a movie, and no one to care how loud I played my music.

"I could do anything," I said in wonder as I strolled through the kitchen. "I could spend the entire month *naked,* and no one would know or care."

I jogged back into the dining room and followed its other door into what I guessed was a library. The walls were covered in shelves, though they held only about a dozen books grouped together on one shelf.

"What a shame," I muttered as I read the names on the books' spines. They were depressingly dull: a few investment guides, a smattering of self-help books with tritely optimistic titles, an encyclopedia, a dictionary, and four novels—all thrillers by the same author. *Good thing I brought my own books.*

Past the library was a study, which seemed to be Mr. Gillespie's domain. Neat stacks of papers sat on the desk, and the walls were hung with large photos of nature scenes. I didn't look any further—partly because I didn't want to intrude on what was probably his personal area, and partly because I had no interest in his job.

Beyond that was a hallway that seemed to lead back to the staircase, then the laundry and a large, empty area that I could only imagine was meant to be a ballroom. I went back to the hallway and looked up and down its length, marveling at the house's size. It felt more like a small hotel than a home, and I tried to imagine the Gillespies living there, only passing each other infrequently in the sprawling building. It held far more space than two people could possibly have needed.

CHAPTER 3
FIRST NIGHT

MY TOOTHBRUSH CLATTERED AS I dropped it into the small blue cup perched at the edge of the sink. I used my hands to scoop the running water into my mouth. Even the tap water tasted different than it did in the city; it was crisper and less sanitized. I closed my eyes, imagining I was drinking from a stream.

My face had become pasty and pale, I noticed as I blinked at my reflection in the mirror. I would have to sit in the sun a few times while I had the chance. My freshly washed hair was beginning to frizz as it dried, and my white pajamas looked too bright against the dull-gray bathroom walls.

"Who paints a bathroom gray?" I asked my reflection. The entire house seemed shrouded by a feeling of gloom, as though the long years had muted and drained its colors. It didn't help that all of the lights were dim, either by design or because of a lack of cleaning, and shadows encroached on the rooms with a cold persistence. I didn't mind too much, though; I found something pretty about the house's dark aura. *In the same way funeral flowers can be beautiful.*

"That's enough morbidity for tonight," my reflection told me. "Bedtime."

I glanced at the stairwell to my left as I exited the bathroom. The wooden steps leading upward disappeared into shadow after the first meter, teasing me with possibilities. I hadn't visited the upstairs rooms yet; figuring out how to start the stove to cook dinner had taken a frustrating forty minutes. Then I'd gotten distracted reading one of the books I'd brought. By the time I closed it, it was well into the night, and I could hear owls calling to each other outside the window.

We'll explore tomorrow.

My room felt welcoming, maybe because of the dozen novels I'd stacked on the desk and beside my bed. I took a final look out the window. The pines' silhouettes stood proudly against the sky as the half-moon cast a thin white light across their tips.

"Good night," I whispered, half to myself and half to the house, then I turned out the light and crawled into bed.

A rasping, scratching noise permeated my dreams, where I walked long hallways without doors. Turning around corner after corner, like a rat in a maze, I chased the sound but never gained on it.

I turned a final corner and saw the hall had led me into a

graveyard. Bleached-white headstones stuck out of the raw dirt like crooked teeth, and when I tried to back away, I found my escape blocked by a cold stone wall.

I woke with a jolt.

The dream hadn't quite been a nightmare, but it had been disquieting, and my heart was racing. I rubbed my hair out of my face and fumbled to turn on the bedside lamp. It took me a moment to realize part of my dream hadn't ended with my waking: a soft scraping sound was barely audible over my ragged breathing. I held still, listening as hard as I could. It sounded like nails clawing at wood.

The cold night air made me shiver as I stumbled out of bed and pulled on my sneakers. I grabbed my jacket out of the wardrobe and tugged it over my pajamas before slinking into the hallway.

The walkway to my left ended in a large window overlooking the woods. The moon cast just enough light for me to see without searching for a switch, so I walked through the house slowly and carefully, searching for the source of the noise. Now that I was listening, a multitude of other sounds crept into my awareness: deep creaking from below my feet; occasional rattling from the floor above my head; then a moaning, grinding sound from inside the wall, where the plumbing became active.

I'd heard it said that some old houses *breathed*, and the Gillespies' building certainly did. The house felt like a living creature, resting in the middle of the countryside, whiling away its years in hibernation. The windows were its eyes, the shingles plated its back. *That would make me...what?*

"A parasite." I snorted in laughter. The sound echoed strangely in the empty hallway. My hand landed on the glass doorknob of the room beside mine, and I gave it a twist just in case. As it had during the day, the lock stayed resistant.

I took the stairwell down to the first floor. The wooden steps whined under my feet as the plumbing farther back in the building gave a final rattle then quieted. The house looked completely different at night. What was dim and dingy during the day became almost luminous under the effects of the moon and stars. The wallpaper seemed more vivid, the wood seemed a richer color, and the secrets hidden in the darkness felt a thousand times more alluring—especially when the shadows writhed across the floor and bloomed out of every corner.

I let myself out the front door without thinking about what I was doing. The desire to see the outside of the building—*the whole of the house*, I thought, *the true house*—had been growing without me even realizing it. Standing on the lawn, I was able to look at its three-story facade. Its black windows watched over the driveway like dark eyes.

Icy dew from the grass stuck on my ankles and the hem of my pajama pants as I walked through it. Like the inside of the building, the outside hadn't been maintained well, and the grass grew thin and too tall. Tiny insects, shocked out of their sleep, flicked away from me as I walked through their homes. A solitary owl called from behind me.

I rounded the corner of the building to have a closer look at the woods. Their branches moved in the breeze, a mess of shadows that could hide innumerable monsters. I looked to my right, away from the woods, and gazed at the side of the house.

My window was easy to find, located nearly at the end of the building, on the second level. I'd left the bedside light on, and the square of glass glowed like a beacon. The window next to it belonged to the locked room. It was different from the others; while every other window in the house sat flush against the wall, that one extended out in a bay shape. I tried to picture it from the inside: there was probably a seat below the window, so that whoever stayed in the room could sit there with an unmatched view of the outside world.

It seemed bizarre that the door was locked. Every other room I'd tried, including the Gillespies' personal bedroom, had been left open. *What's in there?*

I started to lose track of time as I gazed at the window, mesmerized by its possibilities. Everything was so perfectly still that when the curtains fluttered, I actually jumped.

It's just the breeze catching them. I watched the pale shapes hidden behind the glass swirl and sway for a moment before falling still again. The shock had jolted me out of my sleepy daze. I became acutely aware of how cold the wind was and folded my arms across my chest, shuffling on the spot to try to increase the circulation to my numbing feet.

The owl above my head hooted its displeasure at my presence, and I took that as my cue to go back to sleep. *You may rule the world by day, but the creatures of the night demand their privacy.*

CHAPTER 4
SECOND DAY

A FRYING EGG POPPED and spat hot oil at my exposed forearm. I glowered at it and used my spatula to squash the yolk, spilling its golden contents out like blood. "That'll teach you."

Between my midnight excursion and the persistent, grueling dreams of being followed by a scratching noise, I doubted I'd gotten as much as three hours' rest.

Still, it was my second day of solitude, and it had been a welcome change to wake up without hearing the thunder of the tenants in the room above mine as they used their treadmill. *If you're going to jog, at least do it outside*, I'd thought on some of my worse mornings. *Otherwise, you're no better than a mouse on a wheel.*

I flipped my mangled egg onto the plate next to the bacon and sat down beneath the chandelier. The sun was doing a half-hearted job of lighting the house that morning, and I'd had to turn on the lights in order to see clearly. As I ate, I toyed with the idea of going back to bed and sleeping through the rest of the day, but one thought kept me up: I would be able to search the upstairs rooms. The familiar tingle of excited curiosity cheered me, and I finished my breakfast quickly.

As soon as the dishes were dried and put away, I took the stairs to the first floor then turned the corner. I climbed the second flight more slowly, taking my time to savor the exploration. Partway up the narrow stairwell, the wallpaper changed from the sickly gray shade to a dark maroon with intricate gold designs a little reminiscent of the paper in my own room. I reached the landing and found myself in a hallway not very different from the one downstairs. The main change was the lights—or, rather, the lack of them. The only illumination for the hallway came from the square window at the end.

Good thing I didn't try to explore up here last night, I thought as I ran my hand across the patchy, peeling wallpaper. *I would have been as good as blind.*

The wooden floor had a carpet runner down its length. The fabric was scuffed, and the dirty gray base showed through in many patches. Small puffs of dust appeared around my feet as I stepped on it.

An aura of neglect hung over the entire upper level. Dead beetles lay curled in the grime that had accumulated around the skirting. Cobwebs lined the ceiling, though their arachnid occupants seemed to have moved on or died a long time before. As I approached the first door, I noticed even the handle had collected a layer of dust.

It's like the rooms up here haven't been seen in decades.

I brushed the sticky dust off the doorknob and twisted it. The hinges whined and stuck partway through opening, and I had to put my shoulder against the door and give it a good shove to get into the room.

My breath caught in my throat as I gazed at a sea of off-white fabric. The room was filled with furniture, all of it covered with dust cloths. I glanced behind myself, feeling as though Mrs. Gillespie might pop out of the hallway at any moment and reprimand me for snooping. She didn't, so I took a hesitant step into the room and pulled the nearest cloth off its ward, revealing a grand piano made of black wood, with yellowing ivory keys. I reached out and pushed a key down, and a single haunting note filled the room.

"This is gorgeous," I said to the empty room as I ran my hand across the wood. "Why's it hidden all the way up here?" I dropped the cloth back into place and moved on to look at the next hidden treasure.

Beautiful antique furniture filled the room. I found wardrobes, mahogany tables and chairs, two slate-gray mannequins, and pouf seats and armchairs.

My eyebrows rose as I pulled the cloth off a stack of oil paintings near the back of the room. They'd been sat upright, leaning against the wall so I could pull each toward myself to see the one behind it. Most of them depicted people: army colonels with dense gray mustaches; families dressed in Victorian garb; a woman with dozens of strings holding hundreds of pearls hung about her neck; a young, doe-eyed girl who stared out of the canvas imploringly; and a man with a frown set about his eyes as he leaned forward on his desk, reading a letter. The final painting showed an elderly woman, her dark hair streaked gray, her rich maroon dress heavily shadowed. The brightest part of the painting was the large blue teardrop-shaped crystal hung from a necklace, which her right hand caressed as her dark eyes stared out of the painting and transfixed me.

I laid the paintings back into place and rearranged their cloth. I thought about the downstairs rooms and how bare many of them felt. I wondered why such rich—and probably expensive— furniture was hidden in the attic.

The next room was very similar: nearly fifty objects sat about the floor, hidden under dust covers. I set to work exploring them, uncovering dressers, a large box of silver cutlery and crystal glassware, tall-framed mirrors, and boxes upon boxes of moth-damaged blankets and hand-made crochet. By the time I was done, swirls of dust filled the room, catching the sickly light coming through the window, and it was a little after lunchtime.

My back ached, and I leaned against the wallpaper to give it a rest, rubbing dirty hands on my jeans. I tried to picture the downstairs rooms filled with the deep mahoganies and rich curtains. *The gray walls wouldn't look so stark and awful...and that crazy chandelier wouldn't seem so out of place either.*

Had the Gillespies moved the furniture up here, or had they simply never moved it down after buying the house? I hadn't had long to talk to Mrs. Gillespie before they'd gotten into their car and left, but I'd had the impression she'd only lived in the house for a few years. She'd said she missed the city.

I went back into the hallway and paused there, glancing to the left and to the right. I could keep exploring the rooms—there were another two to my left and three on the opposite wall—or I could go downstairs and refuel with some lunch.

The dust was all over my clothes and in my hair, but my desire to look through more of the mysterious upstairs rooms was insatiable. *Just one more, and then I'll take a break.*

I opened the door to my left and felt a rush of disappointment when I saw it was empty. I'd been hoping to uncover more of the gorgeous furniture, but the only thing in the room was a dead mouse, curled on its back with its tiny paws held up toward the ceiling.

My feet kicked up more dust as I walked inside and looked around at the bare walls. I'd been stupid to expect every room to be filled with stored furniture—what I'd already seen was probably enough to comfortably fill most of the house—and I supposed it was a little relaxing to not be cloistered among the ghost-white dust cloths. I held my arms out to the side, stretched my back, then walked to the window to admire the view.

No wonder the light is so bad, I thought as I gazed at the rolling cover of clouds poised above the treetops. Being on the highest floor gave me a slightly better view of the forest. It seemed to stretch on for quite a way. Even though the ground dipped and obscured my view, I guessed it had to continue until it reached the mountains, where fog had gathered several kilometers away.

A door slammed beneath my feet.

I shrieked and leaped backward as I felt the floor's reverberations through my shoes. My left sneaker landed on something lumpy and brittle, which made a faint crunching noise. I scuttled away from it and saw I'd stepped on the dead mouse, squishing it quite a bit flatter than it had been.

My heart thundered. I pressed both hands against my chest, trying to silence my heartbeat while I listened for more sounds from the floor below. *Is someone in the house? Is it a break-in?*

Silence. My fingers shook as they pressed into my blouse. I looked toward the door, which I'd left open a crack, and felt irrational paranoia rush through me. *There's someone in the hallway.*

A hundred thoughts ran through my head. *Can I climb out the window? Should I call the police?* But they became increasingly irrational as fear overrode my ability to think. If I tried to climb out the window, I would undoubtedly fall to my death three floors below, and I'd left my cell phone on the dining table.

I took a halting step toward the door. Icy sweat built under my arms and across the back of my neck. I didn't dare breathe as I took a hand away from my heart and nudged open the door. Half certain that I was about to die, I leaned forward to look into the hall.

It was deserted.

"Get a grip, Elle."

I moved the lower half of my body into the hall too. The hairs on my arms prickled as I faced the stairwell. *What if someone knew the Gillespies were leaving, and came to steal what they could while the house is empty? Would they bring a knife? A gun?* An image flashed through my mind; I saw myself running down the hallway, trying to escape the hulking intruder as he grabbed my ankle, tumbling me to the dust-coated carpet. He brought his butcher knife down to sink it into my chest again and again and again…

"Get a grip," I repeated. I wrapped my arms around my torso, and my mouth was too dry to form the words properly.

I could stay on the upper level until he leaves. I could hide under a dust cloth and pretend I don't exist while he loots the house. Except that I'd screamed when the door had slammed. That wasn't a noise that could be passed off as the house breathing. If he'd heard me, he knew I was there—and he would either flee, or come looking for me.

I turned to the nearest room to my right, where the furniture was covered in yards of off-white cloth. With a final glance at the stairwell, I ducked into the room and pulled the coverings off until I found what I'd been searching for: a crate filled with heavy bronze candlesticks. I picked one up then, holding it like a bat, crept back into the hallway and toward the stairs.

The floor groaned under my weight, and I cursed at it. If the stranger downstairs was listening for me, he would have more than ample warning that I was coming.

Don't be a coward. The Gillespies left you here to mind their house—now mind it!

I took the stairs slowly, my watering eyes fixed on the poorly illuminated landing below, craning my head forward and hoping to see any threat before it had a chance to maul me. My body was alive with adrenaline, and I was becoming dizzy from the excess oxygen my lungs were dragging in to prepare for flight-or-fight.

The landing stayed empty. When I reached it, I looked around the corner. My eyes scanned the shadows that clustered about the edges of the hall, but it was empty.

"I know you're there." My voice escaped as a pathetic whine. I swallowed and tried to put more force into it as I took the first step down the hallway. "I have a gun, but I won't shoot if you show yourself."

I counted to ten, but the only noise was my ragged breathing and racing, overworked heart. There was nothing for it; I took a second step down the hallway, then a third, my eyes flickering over the closed doors, my ears straining to hear any sounds.

The first door to my left was the Gillespies' bedroom. I hesitated, wondering if I should peek in cautiously, but I knew I'd lost any element of surprise a long time ago, so I gripped the doorknob, twisted quickly, then kicked open the door with more force than I probably should have. It banged against the wall then sprang back, threatening to close my view of the room, but I extended my spare hand to keep it open. The room looked empty; the closet door still stood open, as I'd left it before, and the bed had a base that extended to the floor, eliminating any hiding space beneath the mattress.

I backed out of the room and took two more hesitant steps toward the bathroom. "Don't make me hurt you!" My voice was too loud that time, echoing through the hallway and bouncing back at me. I yanked open the bathroom door and stepped into the room, candlestick held high. I caught sight of movement from the corner of my eye and brought the heavy bronze stick down, slashing blindly, but it only hit the shower curtain, which had fluttered in the breeze caused by the opening door.

Back in the hallway, I burst through the second door to the left, the empty storage room. The broom still stood against the wall, looking forlorn.

The next door belonged to the locked room. Tingles ran through my spine as I gripped the doorknob and twisted. Premonition, or maybe superstition coupled with the fear roaring through me, told me to expect the door would open, and I felt a little surprised and disappointed when it didn't.

The last room was my bedroom, and I broke into it with the same burst of energy I'd used to tackle the bathroom, waving my stick at the shadows. It looked exactly the way I'd left it; my books were stacked on the desk and my bed was half-heartedly made. I quirked up the quilt to look between the bed frame and the floor and checked in the closet, but my room was empty.

I wandered back into the hallway, letting the candlestick sag down by my side as I rubbed my dusty sleeve across the sweat that drenched my face.

The noise had definitely come from this floor; it had been too loud and too close to have been on the ground level, and the stairs creaked so badly that I would have heard someone trying to sneak down them.

I looked at the ceiling—yellowish splotches stained the paint around the edges where water had seeped in—and tried to work out where the noise had come from. It had sounded as though it was directly under my feet, and I'd been in the second-to-last room, which was...

Above the locked room.

"Of course," I said bitterly. I walked down the hallway to stand in front of the door and tried the handle a final time. It still stuck.

I got onto my hands and knees, dropping the candlestick, and looked through the crack between the door and the floor. The light was very poor; I remembered the window had curtains over it. Coupled with the cloudy sky, they gave the room a level of light similar to twilight. Even so, I could make out a number of shadowy shapes; the room definitely had furniture in it. I crouched there, straining to see, trying to make out any sort of motion among the swimming shadows.

Then creaks, loud and persistent, rose from the floor below my hands. I pulled back with a jerk and listened as the floor moaned. The noise moved away from me, toward the opposite side of the hall.

I grabbed for my candlestick, fumbled, and dropped it. The brass made a hard metallic *thunk* as it hit the wooden floor.

"Damn, damn, damn it all," I said under my breath, and clambered to my feet, clutching the candlestick against my chest. My heart felt ready to explode.

I took the steps quickly, almost recklessly, against my common sense. Once I was on the ground floor, I turned and scrambled toward the room below the hallway, which turned out to be the library.

The bare shelves seemed much starker and more hostile than they had the day before. The room was U-shaped, with the middle protrusion filled with bookcases. I edged around the perimeter, keeping my back to the shelves as I held up my weapon and checked around the stiff dingy-blue couches and the curtains.

It was empty. I felt lost, so I went back out the way I'd come, into the dining room. I checked the kitchen and the hollowed-out ballroom on the way past then ended up in the living room. I grabbed my cell phone and the slip of paper off the coffee table then hurried to the front door and the safety of the outside.

I didn't start breathing properly until I'd put two dozen paces between myself and the front porch. I stopped under one of the elm trees that flanked the driveway and scanned the front of the building with my eyes. There didn't seem to be any sign of a break-in. Not that there would have been—I'd left the front door unlocked. The only motion I could see came from the bushes and trees that moved lazily in the breeze.

I flopped down in the tall grass and dropped my candlestick. I took a moment to close my eyes and breathe in the oxygen, which tasted sweet and fresh compared to the dusty upstairs rooms. Then I held up the slip of paper Mrs. Gillespie had given me and punched the number into my cell phone.

"Yes?" a cool voice answered after the fourth ring.

"Hi, uh, Mrs. Gillespie," I stuttered, feeling incredibly

underqualified to explain the situation adequately. "I, uh, think someone broke into the house."

"What, Elle?" she barked. "What happened?"

"I was on the top floor when I heard a door slam," I said. "I, uh, went downstairs but couldn't see anyone."

"Is there a car outside the house?" she asked.

I scanned the front lawn as though a car might have materialized in the minute I'd been talking to Mrs. Gillespie. It hadn't.

"No, sorry." I cringed and pressed my palm into my forehead. *Why am I apologizing for the lack of cars?* My brain had shut down under the coldly critical tone coming from the other end of the phone call.

"Don't worry about that then." Mrs. Gillespie sounded suddenly tired. "It would take most of the day to walk up and down our driveway. If anyone was trying to rob us, they'd bring a car."

"But I heard—"

"There's a door in the house that doesn't close properly. It keeps drifting open and slamming in the wind. I've been telling Mark to fix it for years, but...ugh." She stopped herself as if making a conscious effort not to criticize her husband. "Well, it's not fixed yet."

"Oh." I was starting to feel stupid. "There...there were some creaking noises too..."

"It's an old house, honey." Mrs. Gillespie sighed. "The creaks are part of its nature. Unless you saw something or heard someone speaking, I think you're safe."

The stupid feeling was increasing, but with it came a boiling anger. *If there's a door that keeps slamming, wouldn't you tell me about it before leaving me alone in your house for a month? I could have had a heart attack, you stupid—*

"Is there anything else?" Mrs. Gillespie's polite tone carried an undercurrent of irritation.

I searched the rooms! I risked life and limb to protect your damn house! "No, sorry for disturbing you. Have a nice, um, retreat."

She hung up without saying goodbye. I threw down my phone and let myself fall backward, then vented my anger and stress with a strangled scream of frustration. I wished I could teleport back to my apartment, even with its weird smells and obnoxious neighbors…anything to avoid setting foot in the Gillespie house again.

I did the next best thing: I pocketed my cell phone, threw the candlestick toward the front porch, and set out on a walk to burn off some of my agitation.

The clouds gave the yard a bleak, ethereal look. I stopped at the top of the drop-off, just as I had the night before, and looked down at the woods. The incline, dotted with boulders and waist-high weeds, looked strangely inviting, as though I could step onto it and it would carry me in a smooth rush down to the embrace of the light-dappled trees.

I turned back to the house and again saw the bay window, the only thing protruding out from the otherwise-smooth side of the house. The curtains were moving gently from the breeze, but I couldn't see beyond them. I wished I'd asked Mrs. Gillespie what was in there when she was on the phone.

A spotty grove of anemic trees poked out from behind the house. I hadn't seen the complete yard yet, so I started walking toward the outcropping. Past the building's back corner were two small sheds, and beyond those were a series of raised garden beds.

I walked between the knee-high wooden boxes. Many of them still had stakes poking out of the ground, and layers of straw covered some, but clearly, nothing edible had grown in them in a long time. Still tethered to the stakes, shriveled and brittle tomato stalks had been left to die. Even the weeds that had stubbornly grown through the straw looked as though they were one hot day away from death.

It was far more depressing than the inside of the house. I reached the end of the rows and turned back to gaze at them. Someone must have spent hundreds to build the gardens. I couldn't imagine how someone could just...*forget* them like that.

Beyond the garden was a stretch of grass, then the trees rose out of the gully to border the edge of the property. Some sort of building was hidden behind the first cluster of trees; I could see a dark-gray stone pillar and what looked like a roof. Gravel crunched under my feet as I approached the structure to get a better look. The trees were stockier and grew more closely together than those in the forest, and I had to push through meters of the dense, scratchy branches before I reached my goal. Past the trees was a tall, dark wrought-iron fence. A little beyond that were rows of gravestones.

I jumped away from the fence and became tangled in the trees again. I struggled, earning myself a series of scratches across my arms, but I managed to get out, back on the house side of the organic divider. I stuffed my shaking hands into my jacket pockets as I looked from the looming house to the tree-hidden burial site.

The house is big, I thought. *Maybe it wasn't always a private home. It could have been a school or a retirement building at one time.*

That made sense. I mentally counted off the number of bedrooms on the top two floors. The building was large enough to be a small hotel, even.

I turned back to the graveyard, my initial shock waning in the face of morbid fascination. Instead of trying to press through the dense trees again, I followed the edge of the wood, occasionally catching glimpses of iron between the branches. About twenty paces along, the trees thinned, and I was able to reach the fence without much struggle.

The gate stretched at least three feet above the top of my head, and elaborate ironwork swirls and patterns wove down its length. I looked through the bars at the graveyard; beyond the gravestones, a mausoleum rose like a miniature black cathedral, its tar-darkened doors fastened shut with a wooden plank.

The tombstones stood around it in no apparent order. I counted at least a dozen, but more could have been hidden behind the mausoleum. They were all old. Some were cracked; others were nearly toppling over as the ground under them bulged. Two had the entire top halves snapped off, though I couldn't see where the tips were.

"Wow…" I whispered, wishing I'd brought a camera.

The gate was old. Rust ran down it in dark streaks, but it wasn't bolted. I pushed against the left side and was rewarded when it moved inward with a drawn-out screech.

Dirt, leaves, and grime had built up around the base of the gate, and it jammed after moving a foot. The gap was just wide enough for me to fit through, so, casting one final glance at the back of the house, I slipped into the graveyard.

It felt surreal, as though the air inside the gated grounds was heavier. I watched my feet as I stepped between the graves. Unlike the rest of the property, the spaces around the tombstones seemed impervious to weeds. The dry earth cracked in places, and a few errant patches of grass poked out of it, but there were no other plants or greenery.

I looked at the name etched on the nearest stone and stopped short. *Phillipa Gillespie*, it read, its lines faded almost to obscurity.

Is this the Gillespies' relative? The year of death was nearly two hundred years old. *Maybe they inherited, rather than bought, the house.*

The second gravestone had the surname Tonkin, but the one after that belonged to another Gillespie. I moved through the graveyard quickly, checking name after name. I found twelve Gillespies and four Tonkins in total.

A private graveyard, then. I turned toward the house. The highest parts of its roof were barely visible over the tops of the trees. *They must have lived in there over quite a few generations.*

As I walked through the gravestones a second time, I noticed something strange. The birth dates were varied; some were as old as 1795, and the most recent was 1882. All of the death years were the same, though: 1884.

I stalked through the graves, looking for some discrepancy, but there was none. The days and months differed, but every person in that graveyard had passed in the same year.

"What the hell happened here?"

A glint from the direction of the mausoleum caught my eye—a plaque was attached to the door. I approached it and leaned on the thick, rotting wooden plank barring the doorway as I rubbed at the tarnished bronze with my blouse sleeve. It was difficult to read in the poor light, but after some squinting, I was able to make out the inscription.

Here lies Jonathan Gillespie
1840–1884
May the Lord have mercy on us all

"Mercy…" I frowned at the script. "Why would *they* need mercy when *he's* the one that died?"

My skin prickled with unease, and I removed my hand from the wooden barricade, suddenly uncomfortable with touching the tomb. The clouds had grown thicker, darkening the sky. Still, I didn't think the poor light was entirely down to the weather. I must have been in the graveyard for close to an hour, and the sun would soon be skirting over the mountain's edge.

I didn't regret leaving the tombstone-laden field, and I was careful to close the gate behind myself so it wouldn't drift open during the night. Whatever was within those wrought-iron constraints was better off staying there.

A cold wind snapped at me as I hurried around the outside of the house, barely sparing a glance at the locked room's window. I didn't stop until my foot hit the candlestick that had become lost in the long grass around the porch. I cursed, massaging my stubbed toe, then picked up the bronze rod and continued into the house.

Switching on the light didn't do much to fight the gloom, but at least I could see my way into the kitchen. I hadn't paid much attention to my body while I was in the graveyard, but the sight of the fridge made me realize I was starving: I'd missed lunch thanks to the slamming door.

Despite Mrs. Gillespie's reassurances, I didn't want to return to the upper level, especially with the light dimming, so I left the candlestick on the table. I was pleased to see it matched the chandelier nicely.

"Dinner," I coached myself as I plundered the fridge and pantry, "then a shower, then reading, then bed. Don't let the house get to you. This is fine."

I found a red tapered candle in one of the drawers while I was looking for skewers, so I lit it and stuck it in the candlestick. Its floral scent eased my anxieties as I watched the candle burn and ate my dinner in silence.

CHAPTER 5
SECOND NIGHT

THE SLAMMING DOOR WOKE me from disturbing dreams. I sat upright with a muffled shriek, and something heavy fell into my lap. I looked down and saw the book I'd been reading. I must have fallen asleep between pages. My bedside table lamp was turned on but did little to dispel the room's shadows.

Pressing one hand over my thundering heart, I kept still and listened to the house. It was *breathing* again; a pipe rattled somewhere behind me then fell silent. The floor groaned as though weary of bearing its weight. More disturbingly, the scratching noise was back: it scraped, ground, and rasped through the walls around me, setting the hairs on my arms to stand up. The rogue door, at least, had returned to being silent.

It sounded so much louder than the first time, I thought as I made a conscious effort to slow my breathing. *I guess because it's on this floor. It really sounded like it was coming from just behind me, though.*

I felt too jumpy to stay in bed, so I got up, wrapping my robe around myself to protect against the icy night air, and pulled my slippers on. The floorboards groaned under my feet as I approached the room's door and opened it.

Moonlight fell through the window at the end of the hallway, and I drew near to it like a moth to a lamp. The window overlooked the dead gardens, which had become a maze of shadows and dark stakes in the nighttime. Beyond them, I could see the crop of trees that hid the graveyard. I stood there for a while, leaning on the sill and watching the light and darkness play across the ground in response to the trees' swaying. I half-closed my eyes, and I might have believed I was seeing people walk through the woods.

"Enough of this." I rubbed at my arms. "Either go back to bed, or do something productive."

The scratching sound was still echoing in my ears, so I made for the stairwell. It was a risky climb down in the dark, but I made it to the ground floor without breaking my neck. I followed the now-familiar path to the kitchen and turned on lights as I went. A quick search through the pantry turned up cocoa powder and sugar, so I put a saucepan of milk on the stove to heat.

I'd intended to drink the hot chocolate while I read, but when I sat at the table with my book cradled in my hand, I found I couldn't focus on the words. I slammed it shut with a sigh.

The candlestick, with its half-burnt candle, caught my eye.

Why not? I lit the wick and held the bronze pole in front of myself with my right hand, carrying the drink in my left, and strode into the dining room. *Let's explore the house in the dark. We'll make it a proper Gothic adventure.*

The building felt completely different at night, and I looked on it with fresh eyes as the flickering light illuminated a small golden circle around me. Through the dining room, through the suffocatingly empty ballroom, and into the library, I took the chance to appreciate the building afresh.

Something stood out to me as I drifted from room to room. It had been a quiet awareness in the back of my mind since I'd first arrived, but it wasn't until that night, while I was surrounded by smothering darkness, with the only sounds being produced by my footsteps and the house's breathing, that it struck me as strange. The house was neglected, and although the furniture was clean and modern and the living areas were clutter free, there was a peculiar absence of evidence that a family lived there.

I hadn't seen a single photo of the Gillespies, not even in the master bedroom. There were no knickknacks or trinkets, no paintings on the walls, and no furniture that looked as though it was loved. Every single object in the house served a practical purpose, like a hotel room before the guests had unpacked their luggage.

"What does that say about the Gillespies?" I stopped in front of an empty stretch of wallpaper partway down the hall. It was exactly the sort of place that a painting—like one of the gorgeous oil portraits upstairs—would fill perfectly. In fact, as I leaned closer, I thought I could see a square of the wall slightly darker than the rest, as if a painting *had* hung there for many years before being taken down.

Clearly, the Gillespies didn't have the world's happiest marriage.

They were both businesspeople, driven and hardworking, and simultaneously pulled in different directions. What were their evenings like? Did Mr. Gillespie retire to his meticulously clean study while Mrs. Gillespie walked the empty hallways, cleaned out her wardrobe, or worked tirelessly to eliminate any hints that feeling, breathing human beings inhabited the house?

It felt both cruel and crazy that such a rich, soulful building, with its multitudes of rooms and an attic full of decadent furniture, should be dehumanized like that. *Maybe it's a deliberate choice by Mrs. Gillespie. Maybe the house was* too *human.*

I wandered into the library and took my time strolling through the U-shaped room, admiring the bookcases. They seemed to be from the original furnishings; they were a rich, dark wood that shone prettily in my candlelight. They stretched to the roof, offering hundreds of shelves waiting to be filled…or maybe to have their books returned.

A shimmer of movement in the corner of my eye caught my attention. I turned too quickly, and the candle flickered and nearly went out. I froze, waiting as the flame regained its strength, scanning the area that had caught my attention. It was the corner of the inside part of the U-shape. To my left was a straight line to the door that led into the hallway. If I went ten paces to my right, I could turn left again to face the second door.

That suddenly struck me as strange. Why was there an indent in the room that was ten paces wide? What was in that inside section?

I put my half-empty cup of cocoa on the floor, walked around the bend in the library, then exited through the second door to get back to the hallway. I walked the distance between the two library doors, expecting to find a storage closet between them, but it was an empty stretch of wall. Even when I ran my hand across the paint, I couldn't detect any sort of ridge or indent that would suggest a hidden door.

Back in the library, I scowled at the shelves. There had to be something behind them; there was no point in taking so much room out of the library unless it served a purpose. But if a room was hidden behind those walls, it didn't seem to have a door.

I put my candle on the ground beside the cocoa then went to one of the shelves and tried to pull it out. It was fixed in place, either by bolts or cement. I went to each shelf in turn, tugging them so fiercely that I was frightened of pulling a chunk out of the wall, but the only thing my efforts got me was a splinter in my palm. I sucked at it furiously as I regarded the blocked-off area.

"What the hell's wrong with this house?" I asked it. "Locked rooms, and now rooms without doors at all?"

I made to turn away, but a hint of movement attracted my attention again. It had come from the same corner where I thought I'd seen it before. I picked up the candle and moved in to get a better look.

A narrow gap, a centimeter at most, existed between the two shelves that overlapped across the corner. I raised my candle to it and stared into the black depths. There, so close that I could have touched it if the bookcases hadn't been in place, a wide, manic eye stared back.

My mouth opened involuntarily as my body locked up in shock.

I dropped the candlestick and heard the metal ring as it hit the wood floor. The blackness that had been pressing upon me all night overwhelmed me, pouring around my body and threatening to drown me in its icy embrace; then I started stumbling through the black, hands stretched out ahead of me, desperately seeking the exit before the thing in the darkness caught me. My hand hit a wall, and I stumbled then began rubbing my palms across it, searching for the light switch as I became convinced I could hear footsteps creeping through the room, gaining on me, nearly on top of me—

Then I found the switch, and light filled the room. I turned, hands raised to protect myself, but I was alone. The candlestick lay on the floor, still wobbling its way to stillness, its molten tip leaving a splattering of bright-red wax on the floor. The shelves all stood in place; the room inside remained closed.

My idea to explore the house with only the candle suddenly seemed ludicrous. I ran from the library, turning on every switch I passed, lighting up the house like a Christmas tree. Back in my bedroom, I grabbed my cell phone off the bedside table and dialed Mrs. Gillespie's number. It rang twice before her smooth voice answered.

"Thank goodness," I blurted. "There's someone in the house."

"—right now, so please leave a message." The recording finished its greeting then gave a long, angry-sounding beep. I gaped for a moment, at a loss of what to say, then hung up.

It's after three in the morning, I reminded myself as I stalked back down the stairs. *It's not unreasonable to set your phone to voicemail at night.*

I stood in the hallway, faced with a horrible choice. I couldn't leave the house at night. The dirt roads leading to the town weren't exactly clear in normal daylight; if I tried to navigate them in the dark, even with a flashlight, I was more likely to wander into the woods and starve to death than make it back to civilization.

I could call the police, but would they be able to help? There was a room with no door. *What do you expect them to do? Break down the wall?*

Yes, a little, desperate voice in my head said. *That sounds like a dandy idea.*

And yet, I could only imagine what Mrs. Gillespie would have to say when she heard about it. *What were my other alternatives?* I could go back to bed and sleep with the candlestick clasped in one hand…or I could confront whoever or whatever was inside the impossible room.

I hated, hated, hated the choice I knew I needed to make, but there was no way I was going to fall asleep, and I couldn't justify calling the police until I was certain about what I'd seen.

The kitchen drawers held many knickknacks, including potato peelers, zesters, blenders…and a flashlight. I took the thin metal tube out and slowly, cautiously returned to the library.

Everything looked exactly how I'd left it. The candlestick lay on the floor; its wax had dried into a little bloodred puddle. I kicked the stick aside, and it rattled as it rolled along the floor.

"Hello?" I called. Just like that morning, when I'd thought the slamming door had been an intruder, I got no reply. I edged toward the bookcases, turned on the flashlight, and angled it into the gap between the two shelves. "Hello?"

I couldn't see anything, but then, I was still standing farther away than I had been before. I crept closer to the shelves, inch by inch, my heart ready to burst from the pressure, until my nose was just barely touching the wood. I raised my flashlight higher—and saw it.

There was a wall behind the gap in the shelves. On it was a stain that could be mistaken for an eye when seen for a split-second in flickering candlelight.

I thought I might collapse from relief. I sagged away from the shelves, then jumped as the scratching sound started up again.

"Damn it," I hissed as I accidentally kicked the candlestick a second time. "What sort of infestation does this place have? Rats?"

I picked up the candle and the stick, and cast a frustrated glance at the puddle of cold wax that would need scraping off the hardwood. *Tomorrow,* I decided and left the library.

The kitchen clock showed it was nearly four in the morning. I trudged back upstairs to my room, but I could still hear the scrabbling sound. It felt as though it were trying to burrow into my head, to bury itself in a vulnerable part of my brain, and the idea of trying to sleep while encased in that noise made me feel sick. But exhaustion was dragging at me, and after sleeping so badly the night before, I knew I wouldn't do well if I tried to stay awake.

I settled on a compromise and dragged my pillow and blanket downstairs. The living room was quiet, so I bundled up on one of the couches, hugging the pillow and watching the roving shadows until I couldn't keep my eyes open any longer.

CHAPTER 6
THIRD DAY

IT TOOK THREE RINGS for the phone to pull me back to awareness. My pillow flopped onto the floor as I fumbled to pull the cell phone out of where I'd forgotten it in my pocket. I'd become tangled in the blanket overnight and had to kick it off before I could sit up.

"Yeah?" I mumbled as I pressed the phone to my ear.

"You tried to call me last night?" a crisp, cold voice replied.

I squinted against the light coming through the living room window and rubbed a palm against my eyes. "Uh…"

The voice sighed, and I realized Mrs. Gillespie must have gotten a missed-call notification.

"Oh, uh, Mrs. Gillespie. Sorry, I didn't mean to disturb you."

"You didn't," she said curtly, and I could tell she was waiting for an explanation.

I opened my mouth to tell her about the eye I'd thought I'd

seen between the bookcases, but the words died on my tongue. She would think I was being idiotic, of course. I could already tell her patience with me was nearly gone; talking to her about my late-night rovings and hallucinations would do away with it completely, so I seized on the only other explanation I had. "Yeah, there's heaps of scratching noises in the walls. I couldn't sleep."

"Damn it," she spat, almost too quietly for me to hear. "Fine, that will mean the rats are back. You'll need to take care of them yourself. They'll do too much damage if you leave them until I get home. There are rattraps and poison in the storage shed behind the house. Leave them around the kitchen, the laundry, the library, the empty bedrooms on the second floor, and the basement."

My mind was sluggish from sleep. I rubbed at my face, trying to wake myself up and keep track of the instructions. "Right, okay, kitchen, laundry, library…wait, you have a basement?"

The sigh was back, searing me with its irritation. "Yes, of course there's a basement. The door is in the hallway, opposite the conference room."

"Oh. Right."

"There aren't any lights down there, so take a flashlight."

"Sure." My mind fluttered to the other lightless section of the house: the third floor, with its half-explored rooms. I couldn't stop myself from saying, "Hey, there's some pretty old stuff upstairs. What happened with that?"

"You've been up there, have you? Those were the house's

original furnishing. The previous owner put them into storage when he renovated the building. When we moved in, we decided to keep the modern aesthetic."

"That's such a shame," I blurted before I could stop myself. "It's so beautiful—"

"It's old-fashioned," Mrs. Gillespie snapped. "Look, I have to go now. We have a class starting in a minute. Just put out the traps and poison, okay?"

"Sure. Have fun at your class."

Like the day before, she hung up without saying goodbye. I pursed my lips at the phone then put it to one side and stretched. I felt sore from hunching up on the couch, but at least the scratching noise had stopped.

"Jeez, imagine not wanting those gorgeous paintings or chairs," I grumbled as I slouched into the kitchen and put on the kettle. "Why stay in a house like this if you don't like the way it's supposed to look?"

I'd had no idea there was a basement. I must have missed the door in the hallway when I'd explored the lower level.

After breakfast, I changed out of my nightclothes and into jeans and sturdy boots. Then I went outside to find the shed. It turned out to be the first of the two shabby buildings between the house and the vegetable gardens. I got onto my tiptoes to peer through the window, careful not to touch the spider-infested sill. Inside, a jumble of pots, boxes, bags of dirt, and garden tools were piled haphazardly on shelves and the floor.

The door was unlocked but fastened with a rusted bolt, and it opened without too much trouble. I couldn't see any light switch, so the only illumination came from outside and was tinted turquoise by the old window. The smell of organics and dirt filled my nose as I picked my way through the cluttered room.

The rat poisons were in the back, taking up two of the four shelves. "Damn…" I looked at the collection of what must have been nearly a hundred traps and a dozen boxes of poison. "Just how bad is this rat problem?"

There was too much to carry in my hands, so I picked a plastic pot off the ground, knocked it against the shelf to get the dirt and spiders out of it, then filled it with a dozen of the traps. I also took one of the poison boxes then hurried back outside.

Once again, I found myself glancing at the bay window on the second floor as I passed it. The curtains were still, undisturbed by the breeze, and the room's depths were as impenetrable as ever. I looked farther up, above the roof of the house, where the sky was still covered in clouds. The day before had simply been gloomy, but now the clouds were roiling, frothing, and painting the sky a dark gray that threatened rain.

Back in the house, I tried to remember where Mrs. Gillespie had wanted the traps left. *In the kitchen…the laundry… Did she want some put in the library too? Ugh, I should have written it down.*

I ended up leaving a couple of traps and a plate of poison in half the downstairs rooms. When I got to the library, I saw the puddle of red wax on the floor and cringed. The previous night felt as though it had happened a long time in the past, and I suddenly felt incredibly embarrassed for mistaking a stain behind the bookcases for an eye.

When I'd finished setting the traps and poison in the room's corners, I got down on my knees and used a kitchen knife to scrape the wax off the floor. I was lucky the wooden boards were polished; most of the wax popped off in chunks, and by the time I'd finished scraping up the final pieces, it was hard to tell anything had been spilled there at all.

I looked in my plastic pot—I still had four traps left. "That'll do for the basement, I guess."

No wonder I didn't notice the door before, I thought when I finally found it. *It's like a wooden chameleon.* The door, halfway along the hallway that ran down the length of the house, was set between two cupboards and painted the same color as the rest of the wall. Even the handle, a gray-cream plastic, was hard to see.

I juggled my pot and poison box under my left arm then turned the handle and let myself into the stairwell. There weren't any lights, like Mrs. Gillespie had said, so I pulled my cell phone out of my pocket and swiped it on to turn the screen into a makeshift flashlight.

I'd thought the upstairs rooms were dark, but that had been nothing compared to the smothering blackness of that stairwell. I walked slowly, measuring my steps, eyes fixed on the floorboards so I wouldn't trip.

While the edges of the steps were a dark tar-painted color, the centers were worn to a dark sandy shade. *Just how often did people need to come down here?*

I counted the stairs as I climbed. Five…ten…twenty…

At last, after thirty-two steps, the floor leveled out. There was no luxurious dark wood there, only dirt-covered bricks. I scuffed my shoes at the grime, a little disgusted, then raised my cell phone to see the rest of the room.

I'd expected a storage area like the upstairs rooms, possibly filled with boxes and antiques and furniture covered with drop cloths. There was nothing like that in the basement. To my left was a low, wide table, and on top of the table were four stacks of woven mats. The mats were square and about two feet wide. I counted them quickly; there were twenty of them, but I couldn't guess what they'd been used for.

Opposite me, at the other end of the room, was another smaller table. A box and a candlestick sans candle sat on it, and behind it was a chair. Beyond the chair, something large and cloth-covered was fixed to the wall.

The rest of the room was empty.

I paced along the basement's length, phone held out in front of me to ward off the darkness, and stared at the expanse in wonder. It was at least as big as the ballroom, and every surface was covered with thick grime.

I walked around the table to look at the cloth-covered item on the wall. The blanket thrown over it was dirty and had its fair share of cobwebs, though the spiders seemed long gone. I pulled at the corner of the cloth then recoiled as it slid to the ground, revealing its terrible ward to my light.

A giant metal skull, distorted and leering, gazed down upon

the room with empty eyes. At least as tall as a human and built out of dark wrought iron, probably the same iron as what surrounded the cemetery, the metal bones seemed designed as a mockery of what a skull should have looked like. My first thought was that it might have been intended as art, but I couldn't imagine any person who might have wanted such a grotesque abomination in their home. Its position behind the desk, fastened to the wall so that its sightless eyes could watch over the room, made me think it was supposed to serve a purpose.

I thought of the steps, worn down from countless feet. *What was this room?*

My eyes settled on the wooden box sitting on the desk. It was a little larger than my hand, and two metal clasps held it closed. Logic told me to leave it be; the smart, safe thing to do would be to lay the traps and get out of the basement—but curiosity pressed me to open it and see what was inside.

It was a short battle. I put down my mousetrap pot and poison box then flicked up the box's metal clasps. They were rusty and stiff from disuse, but still, they opened. I raised the lid, my heart beating hard from a mixture of fear and anticipation, but my anxiety had been unwarranted. The box was empty except for a slip of paper.

I didn't want to touch the paper, so I lowered my light to read it better. It was written in a neat, precise cursive in what looked like red ink:

The Book of the Others now lies
With Jonathan Gillespie

May the Lord have mercy on us all

"The Book of the Others…" I repeated. "Huh, sounds like a fun read."

I snorted at my own stupid joke, and the sound echoed through the room. Curiosity still niggled at me. *What was in the Book of the Others, and why was it kept in the basement?* However, the leering skull behind my back and the dark, chilly room were making me jittery. I dropped the box's lid closed and hurried to place my traps and poison in the room's corners, then I jogged for the exit and ran up the stairs.

Getting out of the oppressive darkness, even into the house's regular dingy light, was a relief. I closed the door behind myself and went to return the empty flower pot and half-full box of poison to the shed.

The clouds seemed to be darkening. I felt a spit of rain land on my exposed arm and quickened my pace. The shed's door creaked when opened, and I dropped the pot back onto its pile in the corner, replaced the poison box on the shelf, and bolted the door behind myself.

I hesitated then, glancing past the garden beds toward the little cemetery hidden by the trees. *Jonathan Gillespie's final resting place…*

I could return to the house, make a hot drink, put together some lunch, and spend the afternoon trying to purge my mind of the metal skull and empty room below my feet with a good book…or I could try to sate my curiosity about Jonathan Gillespie and why his family had felt they needed to beg for mercy from the Lord.

My mind was made up in a snap. I jogged past the dead, cold garden beds and across the patchy grass until I reached the thicket of trees hiding the wrought-iron fence. Just like the day before, I skirted the edge, looking for the gap that led to the gate. When I found it, I pressed the ancient iron barrier open as far as it would go and slipped into the cemetery beyond.

The stones stood just as I'd left them: worn, cold, and chipped, a last testament to a family that had died within a year of each other. I walked carefully, reluctant to step on any ground that covered a coffin. The air tasted cold and crisp on my tongue.

Jonathan Gillespie's mausoleum stood in front of me, its slate-gray door arched like the entrance to a cathedral. *A church for one.*

A wooden bar stretched across the front of the door, its edges embedded in metal brackets. It was old, eroded by rain and wind, but had been made out of thick, heavy wood.

I didn't want to damage any of Mrs. Gillespie's house, no matter how little she nurtured it, so I took as much care as I could when I set to wiggling the bar out of its brackets. The decayed edges stuck in their holders, so it was harder than I'd expected. I ended up crouching beside one end, putting my shoulder under the wood, and pushing up with all of my strength. The bar groaned, there was a splintering noise, and then it scraped upward, finally coming loose.

I repeated the motion with the other side and was rewarded when the entire bar finally slid free. I pulled it out of its holder and carefully lowered it to the ground. It was heavier than it looked, and it hit the dirt with a hard thud.

My chest was heaving from the exertion, but I was too excited to rest. I put both hands on the icy stone doors and pushed. They gave a little under my hands—not much, a centimeter at most—then ground to a halt. I put my head down and pushed harder, straining every muscle in my arms and back, but the doors wouldn't move so much as a millimeter.

It's locked. I sagged back, resting my hands on my knees as I panted. Something cold stung at the back of my neck; I reached a hand around to feel it was water. The rain had started.

If it's locked, then where's the keyhole? The doors were a smooth barrier with no handle or fingerholds. *It's not…locked from the inside, is it?*

More cold prickles hit my back and arms. The sky above me groaned as thunder rolled through the dense black clouds, and a faint patter in the distance, quickly growing louder, told me it had started raining in earnest on the forest.

"Damn." I bent to lift the wooden bar.

It felt even heavier to get off the ground. I lifted one end first, bracing it on my shoulder and pushing it against the door as the stings of icy water hit me more frequently. I got the first end into place, half inside the bracket, then lifted the other end. My back ached under its weight, but I got it up, pushed it against the door above the bracket, then began to lower it into place.

The doors burst forward with a horrific crack. It wasn't enough to break the seal on the inside, but I felt the cold stone hit my shoulder. I staggered, trying to regain my footing, my ears ringing from the booming sound—but the force had been enough to knock the wooden bar out of my hands. It hit me, throwing me off balance. I fell to the ground. The wood landed on top of me, its edge slamming into my skull just below my hairline.

I lay on the ground, staring at the swirling sky as fat drops of water landed on my face. *How strange,* I thought as shadows crept in at the edges of my vision. *It didn't even hurt that much.*

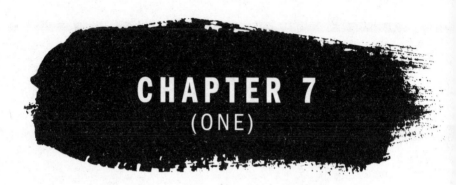

CHAPTER 7
(ONE)

I WAS BACK INSIDE the house, but it wasn't the house I knew. The walls were cleaner and seemed to be a lighter shade of off-white, and the modern furniture had been replaced with stiff wooden chairs and tables.

A girl knelt on the ground in front of me. She couldn't have been more than fifteen or sixteen, but her sallow skin clung tightly to her bones. A thick black dress covered her from her neck to her ankles, and the sleeves extended to her wrists. It had no shape: no frills, bunching fabric, or ornaments. The best word I could find to describe it was *stark*.

She was scrubbing at the floor with bright-pink hands. I walked around her to see her face, and a mixture of pity and revulsion ran through me. Her eyes were sunken, heavy-lidded, and dark. Her limp black hair had been done into a plait that draped over her shoulder, nearly touching the wet wooden floor. Her jaw was a little too thick to make her pretty.

Heavy footsteps reached my ears. The girl must have heard them, too, because her scrubbing became faster, almost frantic, and her eyes widened in fear.

A tall, lean man walked into the room. He stood above the girl for a moment, watching as she scraped the brush's bristles over the wood, then he said, "Let me see."

She drew back obediently, resting on her knees and fixing her gaze on the ground. I saw then that she hadn't been cleaning aimlessly; a dark stain was visible on the wood.

"Rise," he said, and she did, letting the brush hang limply by her side. He walked forward to stand in front of her then gripped her chin in his long fingers. He pulled her face up, forcing her to meet his gaze. "Genevieve, what did I ask you to do?"

"Clean the floor, sir." Her voice was thick and barely above a whisper.

"Is it clean, child?"

"Not yet, sir."

He leaned closer, his eyes boring into hers. "I expect it to be clean by bedtime tonight. You don't want to be punished, do you, child?"

"No, sir." Her voice had a definite tremor.

He released her chin, and she returned her gaze to the ground with evident relief. "Count your blessings, Genevieve. You may take a break now as we commune."

As though on cue, a tall grandfather clock at the back of the room chimed, loud and booming, almost like a church's bell. Genevieve dropped her scrub brush and hurried into the hallway. I followed her and found her standing beside a door I didn't recognize.

Footsteps thundered through the house, and one by one, the rest of the family joined Genevieve—five thin women, three teenage boys, a greasy man, four frightened-looking children, an older, haggard man…

I walked past them, examining equally pale faces and equally dead-looking eyes. The oldest teenage boy's face held a murderously angry look, and he was gripping his left hand. I glanced down and recoiled at what I saw—he was missing three fingers. While the first two stubs looked old and healed, the third stub was raw, red, and barely scabbed over. I reflexively glanced back at the stain the girl had been cleaning. *Surely not…?*

The clock finished chiming, and the gathered family stood stock-still, lined up in a queue. I counted twenty-one of them in all.

The tall man strode into the hallway, his eyes skimming over those gathered before him, apparently checking that they were all accounted for. Then he took a key out of his pocket and unlocked the door.

"May the Lord have mercy on you all," he said as they filed into a stairwell.

I woke with a start. Pain burned across my skull, my limbs felt ice-cold, and rocks and sticks dug into my back. I tried to rise into a sitting position, but something heavy was holding me down. I opened my eyes a fraction, groaning as the pain flared, and saw the mausoleum's heavy plank was lying across my chest.

My body felt sluggish and reluctant to obey my commands. Sharp little pricks were touching all over my exposed skin. I thought they might be pins and needles, but then I realized they were huge, icy raindrops.

I groaned again then put my hands against the plank and began to worm my way out. Soon I was able to pull my feet out from under it and crawl to my hands and knees. Everything hurt, so I sat for a moment, waiting for my head to stop spinning and for the aching to recede. Lightning flashed over my head, and I squinted. For a second, it illuminated the roof of the house standing over me.

I climbed to my feet. I had no idea how long I'd been out, but the ground had become thoroughly soaked by the heavy rain. I stumbled one step at a time across the patchy grass, through the gardens that not even the rain could save, and up the four porch steps.

The house was still and cool. Shivering, I stood in the hallway, dripping rainwater and mud while I tried to get my mind to think through what I needed to do. All I wanted was to lie down on the comfy couch where my blanket and pillow still lay and ease the headache with sleep—but my soaked clothes would ruin the leather, and Mrs. Gillespie would never forgive me for that.

Grumbling, I continued up the stairs and down the hall then let myself into the bathroom.

My clothes were already soaked, not to mention caked with dirt and little bits of nature, so I didn't bother undressing before stepping into the hot shower. I let the flow of water wash the clothes clean, then peeled them off bit by bit and threw them into the sink to dry. I took my time showering. The hot water lessened the headache and eased the muscle pain a little, so I enjoyed it until I was too hot to stay any longer, then climbed out and wiped the steam off the mirror.

A red mark started not far above my right eye and extended to my hairline. *That has to be where the wood hit me.* I reached up and pressed at it, hissing as a flare of pain shot through my skull.

Farther down my body, another mark ran across my lower ribs, where the beam had landed after knocking me out. I didn't think anything was broken, but I guessed it would bruise fantastically.

I wrapped a towel around my body, left the wet clothes in the sink, and shuffled to my room, where I changed into my nightclothes and robe. By the time I got downstairs again, I was functional enough to pay attention to the terrifically fierce force of nature battering the house. The storm had whipped itself into a frenzy; I stopped by one of the windows and twitched the curtain back to see the rain was being driven nearly horizontal, and the barely visible trees in the distance were thrashing like waves.

The storm continued all through dinner, but by the time I had made a mug of hot tea and retrieved the book I was reading, the downpour had settled to a thick drizzle. I sat on the couch, the blanket bundled around me, while I tried to fall into the world of Margot, my novel's heroine. It wasn't easy; she was trying to solve a mystery, but I found I couldn't focus on it while I had such a bleak, infuriating mystery of my own.

That dream I'd experienced when I was unconscious had felt incredibly real—so real, in fact, that I was finding it hard to convince myself it hadn't actually happened. That family, wordlessly obeying the thin man... *What power did he have over them? Why did they put up with his apparent brutality?*

I still hadn't come up with an answer by the time I'd drained the last of my tea. I considered getting up to make another cup, but I was too tired and cozy in my temporary bed to bother, so I lay back and watched the rain create strange patterns on the window.

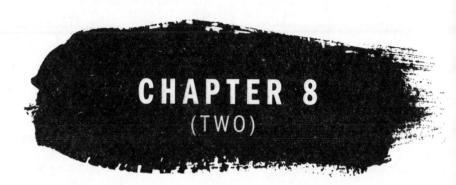

CHAPTER 8
(TWO)

I WALKED DOWN THE stairs with the others, following the tall man's candle. The stairwell led into the basement, terrifically dark and coldly hostile. I heard a scratching noise under the stairs. *Rats?*

The man continued toward the table at the back of the room. His followers—I was sure they were followers of some weird backward cult—each stopped to take one of the mats from the table. They then fanned out along the walls to create a circle, placed their mats on the floor, and sat down.

Unseen, I walked between them, curiously watching the mixed looks of resignation and anxiety on their faces. Once they were all seated, their leader opened the box on the table.

"You're Jonathan Gillespie, aren't you?" I asked him. He neither heard me nor replied. Instead, he took the book out of the box, opened it, and began reading.

"We were begat of darkness, and to darkness, we must return.

The Others who live in the shadows have many gifts to bestow; court their favor, and we will be rewarded handsomely. We will be given *freedom* and see the limits of this mortal world melt away. We will be given *life* and be awake to witness the passing of the millennium. But spurn the Others of the shadows, and you shall feel the sting of their wrath, and you shall know suffering like none other before your spark is extinguished and you are claimed by your grave."

He closed the book with a crisp snap. "May the Lord have mercy on you all," he growled, then blew out the candle, plunging the room into complete darkness. Somehow, I could still see. I glanced up at the ceiling, which doubled as the floor of the room above, where even the thin spaces between the floorboards were filled with plaster.

The family sat shivering in the cold. The youngest children fought their impulses to squirm, and the older family members stared ahead with dead, sightless eyes.

In the dark, insects and rats began to make their appearance. They scuttled between the frozen bodies, obviously familiar with this silent, still circle. Several of the family members closed their eyes as cockroaches crept across their legs.

At the table, Jonathan's cold gray eyes scanned the room, and I was suddenly struck with the idea that he could see in the dark. The twisted metal skull hovered behind him, a reflection of Jonathan's unwavering surveillance.

A rat ran past my feet, and I jumped backward. The room had felt ominous when I'd left the rat traps and poison there that morning—had it really only been half a day ago?—but right then, it felt filled with pure malevolent energy.

The minutes stretched on. *How long does Jonathan expect them to stay down here? How long do* I *have to stay down here?* The atmosphere was making me want to gag.

A rat was sneaking up on Genevieve. She had her eyes scrunched closed against the darkness, but she must have been able to hear the rat, because she flinched when it moved closer.

The rat, no doubt emboldened by the knowledge that the warm beings in its domain wouldn't move, leaped onto Genevieve's leg. Droplets of sweat developed on her cheeks as she recoiled and bit her lip to smother her heavy breathing. The rat climbed her black dress, pausing every few steps to explore and sniff, while tears appeared in the corners of Genevieve's eyes.

I moved closer, wanting to knock the rodent off her, but was powerless to do so. The rat reached her neck; its whiskers breezed over her exposed skin. I glanced at Jonathan. His scowling eyes were fixed on the child; the fingers of his right hand were spread, resting on the table as though he were preparing to stand.

Genevieve finally shrieked. The rat had bitten her; drops of bright-red blood beaded on her neck as she slapped away the mangy beast. Her eyes finally opened, and terror flashed over her face.

Jonathan stood and walked toward her with slow, ponderous steps. The other family members moved their heads to follow his motion, blind in the darkness but listening to the drama that was unfolding.

Genevieve's breathing was shallow and ragged by the time Jonathan stopped in front of her.

"Daughter," he said, and she recoiled at the word, "you've broken the stillness. A punishment is in order."

"May the Lord have mercy on me," she blurted.

"Don't punish her," I begged, standing as close to Jonathan as I dared. "She's only a child! She couldn't help herself!"

Jonathan stared down at his daughter, tortuously drawing out the silence. "You will spend the night here," he said at last. "Maybe some time in our communion place will teach you to respect it."

Relief flooded Genevieve's face, but dread quickly replaced it. Clearly, the punishment was better than what she had feared— but was also worse than she'd hoped.

"You understand why I do this," Jonathan said. He reached out and gripped Genevieve's chin, turning her head up to face him. His voice was softer, almost, but not quite, caring. "Embrace the darkness, and it will give you strength. Embrace it, and it will give you a life many times longer than what you would otherwise bear. But the darkness is not easy to carry; we must practice and show it respect, so that it will grant us these gifts when it deems us ready. You understand?"

Genevieve was shaking like a leaf. "Yes, Father."

Jonathan released his daughter's chin and addressed the rest of the room. "We will return upstairs."

There were several relieved exhalations, and the others rose, picking up their mats.

"Mathilde, you will take over Genevieve's cleaning duties tonight." Jonathan plucked the candle off his table, lit it with a deft stroke, then led the family toward the stairs. Genevieve stayed behind, huddled on her mat as the candlelight faded from sight and the footsteps receded. At last, the door at the top of the stairs clicked closed, leaving the shivering girl alone in the dark.

CHAPTER 9
THIRD NIGHT

"NO!" I SPAT, JERKING upright. Pain seared across my temple again, and I pressed my palm to it, waiting for it to ease. Confused and disoriented, I took a moment to realize I was still in my makeshift bed in the living room. I groaned, pulled myself to my feet, and wrapped the blanket around my body.

I must have been asleep for hours; night had coated the house in darkness, and I groped for the light switch. I stumbled out of the living room, where the wooden floor was cool on my bare feet, and into the hallway.

I had to let the girl out. She was trapped, frightened, and surrounded by the rats and insects, and her father planned to leave her there all night. I could help her, though. I *had* to help her.

The door was so well concealed that I nearly ran past it. It was so different in my dreams; the wooden entry had been tall and dark then, filled with power and importance.

I opened the door and looked into the black stairwell. "Genevieve?"

Idiot, I thought as my voice echoed back at me from the void. *It was a dream. Genevieve isn't real.*

It had *felt* real, though, so much more real than anything else that had happened to me that day, so I hurried into the kitchen and retrieved the candlestick from the table, lit its blood-red candle, and returned to the unholy basement.

The room was almost exactly the way I'd left it at the end of my dream. Only the cloth thrown over the iron skull and the empty floor were different. No Genevieve.

"Of course," I muttered, more than a little angry at myself for being so impulsive. *It was only a dream. Genevieve is probably your brain trying to send you a subconscious message to stop reading horror or something.*

Even so, I found it hard to convince myself that Genevieve didn't need my help. I turned, preparing to climb the stairs again, and glanced upward. The cracks in the ceiling were filled in with plaster.

One hand on the banister and my right foot on the first stair, I was rooted to the spot. That little detail—the plastered ceiling—had been in my dream. Jonathan had filled in every last gap so that no light could find its way into his homage to darkness. But how could that be in a dream if I'd never noticed it before?

My mouth opened a fraction, and I frowned, trying to reconcile the knowledge. Maybe I'd subconsciously noticed the ceiling, and my brain had slipped it into the nightmare. And yet, it wasn't something I would have noticed unless I was looking for it. *Then why…?*

The door snapped closed.

I jumped and stared at the place that had once been my escape. A gust of wind followed the door's motion and caught my robe, chilling me. My candle's flame died with a quiet hiss.

I swore then started running. *Am I trapped? Does the door lock itself?*

Pain shot into my foot from where I stubbed my toe, but I didn't slow down. I imagined myself as Genevieve, trapped in the lightless, heatless basement, fighting off overly bold rats and clicking insects, waiting for a rescue that would come months too late.

Terror made it hard to think as I reached the landing and felt blindly for the door—which had no handle.

"Damn, damn, damn," I panted, exhaling the word with every breath. I scrabbled around the edge of the door, my fingernails trying to find purchase, ignoring the stings of splinters. I thought I heard a skittering sound behind me.

Genevieve's face rose in my mind—her wide, terrified eyes pleaded with her father as he left her in the room, dread painted across her face as she watched her family climb the stairs. I felt her eyes on me, observing me, her companion in her cruel jail.

"No." I backed up as far as I could. Then I started running, angling my shoulder at the door, and hit it as hard as I could.

I burst through it, splinters of wood shooting into the hallway in my wake. My knees gave out, and I collapsed to the ground, panting and clutching at an anxiety-induced stitch. For a moment, I didn't move. I knelt there on the wooden floor, savoring the sight of the poorly lit hallway and rooms, feeling the burn on my shoulder. *Guess that'll be another bruise.*

When I turned back to the door, I saw I hadn't broken it completely, as I'd assumed. I'd merely cracked the wood around the crude lock.

"Jeez," I muttered, gaining my feet and dusting off my robe. I felt wobbly, and my headache was back, throbbing at my skull. The room had made me jittery and anxious, and I didn't like the way the black stairwell was left exposed, so I shoved the door closed then backed away from it. "You're sick, Jonathan Gillespie."

It felt good to be able to say it, to express that hatred and revulsion that his family had been incapable of verbalizing. I stumbled to the kitchen, *his kitchen,* and put the kettle on. I glanced down and saw I still had the candlestick clutched in my hand, though the candle had broken in half during my escape. I dropped it on the table.

A glance at the clock showed it was a little after midnight. I didn't feel tired, so I jogged up the stairs to fetch my laptop, and I had it plugged in at the dining table before the kettle had finished boiling.

I typed Jonathan Gillespie's name into a search engine. I wasn't sure what to expect, but I was disappointed all the same. The first page of search results brought up nothing but social media profiles, an article about a Canadian lawyer, and a steamy romance novella whose hero was unfortunate enough to share Jonathan's name.

I didn't hold much hope for it, but I clicked through to the second page. The first few results were more of the same, but the fourth link took me to a blog run by someone named Steve Gillespie. The blog seemed to be full of discussions on poetry, classic movies, and half-baked philosophical thoughts. Judging by his profile picture, Steve was well into the latter part of his life, and the blog hadn't been updated in nearly five years. I did a search for Jonathan and found a post called "Some Ramblings for Posterity" that seemed to be talking about the same Jonathan who had once owned the house.

Steve's writing style was slow and confusing, and he took frequent detours to wax lyrical about his childhood. I skimmed the massive post, trying to pick out the parts that seemed relevant and reading between the lines when Steve wasn't clear.

Steve was apparently Jonathan's grandson. While he'd never met Jonathan, his mother had told him enough stories to fill in the details. He described growing up in a beautiful house, but it wasn't until he mentioned a graveyard hidden in the woods out the back that I realized he was probably talking about the very building I was staying in.

According to Steve's mother, Jonathan Gillespie had once been a cult leader. He'd amassed a following of nearly a hundred, though a reasonable number of those were his multiple wives and many children. When his followers had tried to rebel against him in 1871, they had fallen to a "great calamity."

"What sort of calamity?" I scrolled on, but Steve either didn't know or didn't think it important enough to elaborate on.

Instead, he speared off into a cute side story about the pet dog he'd owned that would fetch his shoes, but only in mismatched pairs.

I kept reading, and soon the story picked up again. After the "calamity," Jonathan and his remaining family—three wives, his sister and her husband, his two brothers, and their many children—had packed up and left. He'd led them over the mountains, where he'd lost a number of the children to the harsh conditions, and eventually arrived at an unoccupied stretch of land a few hours' walk from a small town.

There, his family spent months building a house to Jonathan's exact specifications. Steve noted that Jonathan Gillespie had been incredibly particular about how the house was built but didn't say why.

"C'mon, Steve," I begged, scrolling past another anecdote about the time he'd misheard his mother and purchased a bunch of flowers instead of the bag of flour he'd been sent to the store for. "C'mon, don't leave me hanging like this."

Steve claimed Jonathan had ruled his family with an iron fist, which, if my dreams had been even slightly accurate, was true. Each day, they would "commune" for an hour. While Steve didn't elaborate on what this communing was, I guessed it was the bizarre scene I'd witnessed in the basement.

There was a mention of Jonathan watching from his window, which had the best view in the house, while his family worked the gardens. Steve then finished his story by saying Jonathan had gotten his just deserts for his cruelty; he'd been the first to fall to the mysterious illness that had "wiped out nearly all of the Gillespies and Tonkins." I remembered the smattering of gravestones with the name Tonkins. They probably belonged to Gillespie's sister, her husband, and their children.

Obviously, at least some of the Gillespies had survived—otherwise, Steve wouldn't have existed to tell his story—but the frustrating narrator hadn't said how many.

I thought of Mr. Gillespie, obviously a great-grandchild or great-great-grandchild of Jonathan. I wondered how much he knew about his family history. I was tempted to call and ask, but I'd never spoken much with Mr. Gillespie beyond hello and goodbye. Mrs. Gillespie had organized all the arrangements for my stay, and even if she knew anything about her husband's ancestors, I doubted she was willing to talk about it.

I spent another forty minutes looking through other search results in case Jonathan had another descendant who was a little more coherent about his history, but I gave up when I reached page twenty-seven, which was full of gibberish results.

The clock read two thirty in the morning, but I was still too energized to sleep. I made another cup of tea and fished leftovers out of the fridge for a midnight snack while I processed what I knew. The Gillespie house had been built nearly two hundred years before by a cult leader. He'd created it to serve a specific purpose, which I had yet to discover. Steve Gillespie had implied that his grandfather had somehow been involved in the deaths of his followers and a number of his family before moving, but I couldn't guess to what degree Jonathan had caused those deaths.

Steve's brief mention about Jonathan watching his family through his window had given me pause. While he hadn't elaborated on where it was in the house, my thoughts were instantly drawn to the bay window of the locked room on the second floor. Because it jutted out of the wall, it had the best view in the house. On the other hand, it only overlooked the gully that led to the forest, whereas the gardens were behind the property, out of view of even the bay window.

Except...

I thought of the raised beds behind the building. They were old and definitely dead, sure, but they were nowhere near as old as the house was.

What if the garden was originally around the side of the house, where there's more sunlight? That would put the garden right under the bay window. I pictured Jonathan standing in the gap between the curtains, his cold gray eyes watching his wives and children toiling in the dirt below...a pair of clippers gripped in his fist, perhaps, ready to punish anyone who showed signs of disobedience.

I snapped my laptop closed and picked up my cup of tea, eager for the comfort of the warm drink. The rain was still coming down, tapping along the windows and thundering over the roof.

Sometime between falling asleep on the couch and forcing my way out of the basement, I'd come to cautiously accept my dreams as more than complete fiction. They had a sense of realness and coherency that my regular dreams never even got close to, and they were showing me things that were being confirmed by reality.

What scared me most was that I didn't know where the dreams were coming from. *Is it the house?* I'd thought on more than one occasion that it had felt alive. *Or is it something residing* in *the house?*

And why me? Did I have some latent psychic ability I'd never known about? Were there ghosts within these walls, trying to communicate with me? I'd never really given much thought to spirits or the afterlife, but after what I'd been through over the last three days, I was finding it hard not to believe in them.

I thought about Genevieve, with her thick jaw and sallow skin, and remembered the terror that had flashed over her face when she'd been locked in the basement. *He did let her out, didn't he?*

Thunder crashed. I pulled the blanket around myself more tightly and drained the last of my tea.

Something was *wrong* in the house, and I had the feeling it all stemmed from the locked room on the second floor. I stood up to put my cup in the sink and nearly dropped it as a door slammed above my head.

"Damn it!" I snapped reflexively, pressing my free hand to my heart. No wonder Mrs. Gillespie needed marriage counseling if her husband refused to fix that abominable door.

I put down my cup and adjusted the blanket around my shoulders. It was late—or rather, early—and I was letting my imagination run away on me. I probably just needed a few hours' sleep, and maybe a couple of painkillers for my aching ribs and throbbing head, and I would be fine.

The floorboards above my head groaned. I hesitated, listening to them, trying to remind myself that it was just the house breathing…

Except it wasn't. They weren't random creaks; they were footsteps in the hallway above me.

It was a good thing I'd put down my mug; otherwise, I would have dropped it. Panic flared through me while my brain tried to reason against it. *There can't be anyone there. You would have heard them come in.*

The footsteps kept moving, starting to the left and traveling directly over my head.

There's no one there. The house breathes; that's all.

They'd changed direction and were heading down the hallway, toward the back of the house.

You're safe. You're safe. You're safe. I ran for the stairwell, clutching the blanket in one hand and the candlestick in the other. The stairs tended to creak, so I kept my feet light and stayed to the edge of the steps, minimizing the noise the best I could.

The landing was empty and dark. I glanced up the stairs behind me, the one that went to the third floor of the building, but there was no noise coming from there, so I faced the hallway in front of me and began advancing down it.

The doors were all still open from when I'd searched them the night before. I glanced into each room as I passed but saw no sign of an intruder. I eventually reached my own room and looked inside. It was exactly the way I'd left it. My pile of novels, which I'd barely made a dent in, still sat on the table. My closet door was open from when I'd gotten my robe, and the bed looked bare without the blanket that I was currently clutching around my shoulders.

Then the scratching started again. I held still, listening hard, and realized it was coming from the wall behind my bed. I moved close and pressed my ear against the cool wallpaper.

The more I listened, the less I was convinced that rats were the cause.

I pulled back and jogged into the hallway again, my heart thundering in my ears, trying to drown out the dreadful scratching sound. The noise was coming from the room next to mine—the room with the locked door. *The room that belonged to Jonathan Gillespie.*

Even though I knew what the result would be, I couldn't stop myself from trying to turn the handle. Still locked.

Why?

I ran down the stairs, hardly thinking about what I was doing, and dropped the candlestick in the hallway before pelting out the door and into the rain. It was achingly cold and soaked through the blanket before I'd even rounded the corner. Visibility was poor, and I couldn't hear much over the roar of the drops assaulting the house and the muddy, slushy ground, but I kept marching down the side of the house until I stood below the bay window. I pulled out my phone, grateful that it was waterproof, and turned on the flashlight function. The room was a long way above me, but the phone's light was just enough to let me make out the window.

The curtains fluttered in the breeze for a second before falling still. Dread pooled in my chest like molten lead as the implication hit me. *There is no breeze…not in the hallway, not outside.* The rain was heavy, but the wind had settled, letting the drops fall directly down. I watched the window with a dry mouth. *Is someone living in there?*

Impossible. I'd been in the house for three days. Even if someone had food and water in the room, they couldn't go to the bathroom without my knowing. *Right?*

The dreams…what if there was a spirit in the house, trying to show me something or teach me something? Or what if Jonathan Gillespie's ghost was still trying to rule over the home that had once been his?

I needed to open the door—to see what was in the only locked room in the house. *How, though?*

I could call Mrs. Gillespie to ask where the key was…and, most likely, endure her scorn before being told that I shouldn't pry where I wasn't wanted. Or I could force my way in. I'd already broken the basement's door; Mrs. Gillespie wasn't likely to get *that* much angrier if I broke a second one.

That settled it. I jogged toward the sheds at the back of the house, shoved open the spider-infested door, and shone my phone's light at the clutter on the ground and shelves. Sure enough, in the corner, among shovels, pruners, and tree saws, was a rusty crowbar. I kicked the clutter out of my way and grabbed the bar, shook it to detach it from the cobwebs, then ran back into the rain.

This is crazy. I skittered through the front door, dropped my soaked blanket on the ground, and took the stairs two at a time. *But sometimes crazy circumstances warrant crazy actions.*

I didn't stop moving until I reached the locked door, where I stumbled to a halt, bent over, and braced my hands on my knees to drag in a few rough breaths. A stitch had developed in my left side, and my throat was dry from the stress and the running.

I listened hard, but everything was still and silent again. Even the scratching sounds had stopped; all I could hear was rain drumming on the roof. I knelt, pressed my cheek against the wooden floor, and shined the light from my phone under the door.

Just as I had on my first day in the house, I could see faint outlines of objects I couldn't make out, but there was no sign of motion and no hint of what might have been inside.

"We're really doing this, huh?" I picked up the crowbar and fit its angled edge between the door and the doorframe. For a second, I hesitated, wondering if I should leave the task until morning and maybe call Mrs. Gillespie to see what her excuse was, but the tension had built so strongly in my chest that I thought I would explode if I didn't get an answer right then. "I guess we are."

I heaved on the crowbar. The wood creaked, then I was rewarded with a faint cracking noise. I pushed harder, the stitch stabbed at me again, and my headache flared. Then the wood gave out under the pressure with a splitting crack, and the door finally swung open.

CHAPTER 10
FOURTH DAY

I STOOD IN THE doorway, blinking and gasping, trying to orient myself and make sense of what I was seeing.

Plenty of scenarios had flashed through my mind in the days and moments before I'd opened the door, but none of them came even remotely close to reality.

My optimistic side had hoped for an empty storage room, like the one to its left; locked, maybe, because the window didn't close properly and the Gillespies were trying to stop the breeze.

My pessimistic side had pictured an evil lair filled with replicas of the wrought-iron symbol in the basement or corpses stacked along the walls while the room's occupant laughed at my foolishness for walking into his trap.

What I saw was worlds away from either idea.

I turned the light on as I walked through the doorway and gazed about the room. To my left was a small bed—too small for an adult—with a pink floral comforter. A child's rocking chair sat beside it, a stuffed bear posed in its cushioned seat. To the right was a wardrobe set into the wall, much like the one in my room, except this one had posters of horses taped to it. A deluxe dollhouse—so big and complex that a younger version of myself would have cried from jealousy—was propped below the bay window.

I hadn't been able to see from the outside, but the window's curtains were actually pink with frilled edges. The windowsill was painted white, matching the other accents in the room that set off the pastel-peach walls.

A stack of boxes, all open, sat in the middle of the room. I caught glimpses of a diary, a photobook, and a collection of picture frames inside.

"Wow…" I remembered that this was supposed to have been Jonathan Gillespie's room, and I broke into laughter.

It was such a relief, so much sweeter and less menacing than what I'd feared, that I let myself fall to the ground and raked in gasping breaths between bouts of chuckling. After a few minutes, I calmed down—and looked at the room with fresh eyes.

I'd found out its terrible secret, which wasn't that terrible to begin with, but that didn't explain why it had been locked. I scooted over to the box holding picture frames and pulled out a few.

They showed Mr. and Mrs. Gillespie, looking a little younger, posed with a girl with shoulder-length straw-colored hair. She had a huge gap-toothed smile, and I guessed she wasn't older than six or seven.

I pulled out more photos, and they were all variations of the same. The Gillespies with their daughter at an amusement park. Mrs. Gillespie pushing the toddler on a swing. A Christmas photo that was marked from five years previously.

If this was the Gillespies' daughter, where was she now?

The Christmas photo looked like the most recent. The child was holding up a miniature toy horse, beaming at the camera while Mrs. Gillespie sat on the ground just behind, wearing longer hair and holding a glass of wine. The date set it at five years before, but the girl couldn't have been older than seven. *That would make her a young teenager now.*

Where is she? Boarding school? Mr. and Mrs. Gillespie seemed the sort of people who might send their daughter to one. I knew I was pushing the limits of what was appropriate, but I was too curious to stop. The second box held stacks of newspaper clippings, and I pulled out a handful. The headline on the top sheet—from January five years ago, not long after the Christmas photo—made my heart drop: *LOCAL GIRL MISSING.*

I skimmed it quickly. The Gillespies' child, Hanna, had been reported missing on the morning of January 18. It was a suspected kidnapping, and the police were asking for information.

More of the story unfolded through the clippings—there were at least thirty of them, stacked in chronological order. Police had searched the house and found no signs of a forced entry, and all the footprints in the damp ground had matched the Gillespie family's shoes. However, a set of footprints belonging to Hanna had led toward the forest, though no one was sure how old they were.

Nearly a hundred police officers and volunteers had spent three days scouring the woods. No signs of Hanna were found, and the search was eventually scaled back then called off completely. Mrs. Gillespie believed her daughter had been kidnapped, rather than lost. She made repeated requests for information in the media. Two weeks after her daughter had disappeared, she offered five hundred thousand dollars to anyone with information that led to her daughter's discovery. Despite hundreds of leads, Hanna wasn't found.

The last clipping was from four months before the Gillespies left me in charge of their home. It was the four-year anniversary of Hanna's disappearance, but Mrs. Gillespie still hadn't given up. The reward was still on offer, she said. She implored the police to pull the file out of storage and reassess it, and she pleaded with the public to come forward with information. The article quoted her as saying she couldn't rest until her child had been found. A photo was included, showing what Hanna might look like at age eleven.

I carefully put the clippings back in the box in the same order I'd found them, then I looked around the room again. My stomach turned leaden as I realized what it was: a shrine to the Gillespies' lost child. Of course the door had been locked; the room was private, special. They hadn't wanted intruders poking through their missing daughter's possessions…which was exactly what I'd done. I stood up, feeling ashamed and a little sick. The room held the Gillespies' private grief, probably the reason their marriage was failing, and a virtual stranger had beaten down the door and riffled through their daughter's memorabilia. I intended to back out of the room, close the door, and never open it again, but something stopped me.

Did the Gillespies know the room had once belonged to Jonathan Gillespie? *Surely not.* They would have chosen the room for their daughter because of the beautiful bay window that overlooked the gully. They couldn't have known their child's room had once housed such an evil man…*no, not a man—a monster.*

I looked back at the photo frames, at Hanna's infectiously free smile, and my skin crawled. She'd been a descendant of Jonathan Gillespie, a cult leader who believed there was power in darkness and death, and she'd lived in his room.

The police seemed to think Hanna had woken up early on the morning of her disappearance, gone for a walk, and become lost in the woods. But I had a horrible, sinking idea that Jonathan had somehow been involved.

"That's crazy," I told myself, my eyes darting around the peach-and-white room. "He's been dead for nearly two hundred years. You've lost your marbles, Elle."

And yet, I couldn't summon the willpower to leave. Instead, I knelt back in front of the second box, which held a collection of Hanna's toys. A leather-bound book was hidden just below a pack of horse stickers.

"I shouldn't be doing this," I said as I gently extracted the diary. "This is so, so wrong."

The police had probably already been through the room five times over, I reasoned as I opened the diary to the first pages. As much as I felt as though I was violating the Gillespies' privacy, I certainly wasn't the first person to do so.

The diary was filled with a child's scrawl. Hanna had been a reasonable speller, but she hadn't bothered trying to keep the words within the faint lines scored on the paper. Her sentences rolled across the surface in whichever direction they decided to go. It made reading difficult, but I got the gist of the first entry: she'd been given the diary as a present when they moved into their new house.

New house...this house?

She wrote about choosing the room with the big window and lining her toy horses on the sill so they could look outside while she slept.

I flipped through the pages, picking up on bits of trivia while I looked for anything that could correlate with my suspicions. A few months after moving in, Mr. Gillespie had hired contractors to build garden beds out the back. Hanna had helped him plant seeds and had watered them every morning. A few entries after that, she'd stumbled on the cemetery, but her parents wouldn't let her go in. Her parents had plans to repaint the entire house and buy more comfortable furniture—but it looked as though Hanna's room was the only one that had been spruced up.

Then I saw something that made me pause. Hanna had written about "little voices" talking to her through the walls. She thought they were fairies that were hiding from her. According to Hanna, they didn't speak English, but they would sometimes reply when she spoke to them.

I turned the page, eager for more information, and found it was empty. I flipped further, searching for more of the winding scrawl, but there was nothing else in the diary. Frustrated, I turned back to the last page and checked the date: January 16, just two days before she was reported missing.

It felt as if a bucket of cold water had been poured over my head. Guilt for looking through the lost girl's possessions drew over me, and I reverently put the diary back in the box then scooted backward until I could rest my shoulders against the wall.

I didn't like the idea of voices talking to the girl. Had she told her parents? Had Mrs. Gillespie replied, just as she'd told me, that it was "only the house breathing"?

As I struggled with the new knowledge and fought to put the puzzle pieces together, I barely noticed as my eyelids, weighted down by missed sleep, fell closed.

CHAPTER 11
(THREE)

"I'M GOING TO DO it." Genevieve's heavy eyes were wide as she crouched beside a bed. I stepped forward to get a better view and saw a sleepy figure stirring in the sheets.

One of the other girls, slightly older than Genevieve but with the same thick, black hair, propped herself up and rubbed at squinted eyes. "Wha…?"

"I'm doing it tonight." Genevieve's voice was hoarse with excitement and fear. "What we talked about. Remember?"

That got the other girl's attention. She sat bolt upright, and her face turned pale. "But you… How?"

The room, which I recognized as the same corner room I slept in, had two beds. The one opposite—Genevieve's, I guessed—was neatly made and hadn't been slept in, even though Genevieve was wearing a long white nightdress.

"I'll follow him to his crypt," she replied, speaking quickly.

"He's been going there every night for the past week and doesn't come out for hours, remember? I think he's trying to get the darkness to convert him. He'll go there again tonight, I'm sure of it, and I'll follow and lock him in."

The other girl looked terrified. "If he catches you, he'll kill you."

"He's killing us anyway," Genevieve snapped back. "Just far more slowly."

The sisters were silent. I listened to the house as it creaked and breathed.

"You don't think Mother will let him out?" the older one asked at last.

"She won't be able to if I hide the key."

"Do you want me to come?" Even I could pick out the reluctance in her voice.

"No, I'm doing it alone. I just…I wanted someone to know, in case I don't come back."

"Yes." The older girl stroked Genevieve's face, brushing her hair out of it. "Good luck."

As Genevieve stood up and walked toward the door, I finally saw her face properly. I'd thought she wasn't very pretty before, with her sallow skin, thick jaw, and heavy lids, but in that moment, I thought she was breathtaking. Her cheeks were tinged pink from excitement, and her eyes, though still heavy-lidded, burned with a blistering determination. No matter how meek she appeared in her father's presence, she had an intensity inside of her that took my breath away.

I jerked awake. Light hit my eyes, making me squint and blink while I tried to collect myself. I was still in Hanna's room, I realized, surrounded by the missing girl's toys, clothes, and decorations.

"Jeez," I muttered, awkwardly clambering to my feet. I felt disoriented, as though I'd fallen through a portal into a different world.

The rain was a steady drizzle, leaving trails on the window. I couldn't tell how much time had passed or whether I'd fallen asleep completely or just dozed, but my neck was sore from where my head had lolled.

I suddenly felt very uncomfortable in the room—ashamed, even. I stood, backed out of the door, and closed it behind myself, cringing at the sight of the splintered wood around the lock. That was two doors I'd broken in the Gillespie house, and one of them without good reason. I felt horrible.

To the right was the window at the end of the hall that overlooked the gardens. I approached it, leaned on the sill, then gazed over the lawn at the shrubby bushes that hid Jonathan Gillespie's graveyard. Was this where Genevieve had stood that night to watch her father make his way toward his mausoleum, waiting for her chance to lock him in?

What was he even doing down there? I thought back to the day before, when something had shoved from the locked inside of the mausoleum, bowing the doors out and knocking the wooden plank on top of me. I couldn't even guess at what sort of force was necessary to do that to solid granite doors. Much more than was human, I suspected.

I realized I'd never put the plank back in place. *Was there a reason it was locked on each side?* I'd assumed the wooden barricade was there to protect the mausoleum from vandals, but what if it was meant to protect the house from whatever was inside the crypt? I shivered, feeling sick. *What should I do? Should I call someone? Who would possibly believe me?*

I took the stairs down and checked the kitchen clock. It was nearly midday. I'd been up almost all of the night, except for when I'd nodded off in Hanna's room, and felt ghastly for it.

As I turned on the kettle and prepared a simple lazy sandwich made from frozen bread, pickles, and cheese, I couldn't stop myself from thinking of Genevieve. I wasn't sure how I felt about her anymore. She'd been planning to kill her father. That should have made me hate her, but…all of my hatred was already directed at Jonathan Gillespie. If anything, I admired Genevieve for what she'd done…whether she'd succeeded or not.

I desperately wanted her to have won. As I ate my sandwich, I realized there was something I could do to find out the answer: sleep. The last three times I'd closed my eyes, I'd seen a slice of Genevieve's story, and I had the feeling the same would happen next time I laid down for a nap too.

The couch looked very appealing at that moment; I felt wrung dry from tiredness, but at the same time, I wasn't prepared to fall back into Jonathan Gillespie's world. I was terrified of what I might see if Genevieve had failed.

Instead of sleeping, I took my time washing the plate then climbed the stairs and took a shower.

The bruises looked worse, if anything, but they felt a little less tender. I dressed then stood in the middle of the hallway, scanning the rooms, trying to think of a job that would keep me awake.

Almost without deciding to, I found myself climbing the stairs to the third floor. It had been dim the last time I'd been up there, thanks to the lack of electric lighting, but now, with the storm blocking out almost all natural light, it was nearly impossible to see. I moved slowly and carefully as I walked through the rooms and reverently brushed my hands over the covered furniture.

This furniture hadn't existed during my dreams, I realized. The Gillespie house in Jonathan's time had been furnished spartanly, with neat but uncomfortable wooden chairs and basic tables. The ornate furniture and crystal glassware must have come later.

The paintings at the back of the room attracted my attention. I pulled off their cloth and began flipping through them again, admiring the scenery paintings, but paying especially careful attention to the portraits.

If I wasn't mistaken—and I was certain I wasn't—the subjects were descendants of the Gillespie line. I saw a few heavy-lidded eyes, pale skin, and a lot of dark hair. They looked healthy, at least, and I felt relieved for it.

I pushed the paintings back into place as my mind went to the little cemetery at the back of the property. Every gravestone had been placed there in the same year.

What does that mean?

I clambered down the two flights of stairs and out the front door. It was still drizzling. I took a deep breath, jumped down the porch steps, and jogged around the side of the house. I couldn't stop myself from glancing up at the bay window as I passed. The curtains really looked gray from the outside, but that was probably thanks to the poor lighting. At least they were still.

I kept up the pace as I ran past the dilapidated shed, the dead vegetable gardens where Hanna had probably nurtured the now-dead tomato plants, and toward the thicket of trees beyond.

Mud had splashed up to my knees and my clothes were drenched by the time I pushed the high iron gate open and walked into the cemetery. The gravestones stood like sentinels guarding the mausoleum. I dragged in a deep breath and began to walk reverently through the family's final resting places.

The deaths had all occurred between March 1884 and November 1884. Some of the graves housed middle-aged men and women, but many belonged to the children and teenagers.

I went through the graveyard twice, reading each name aloud, before I was satisfied: Genevieve hadn't been buried there.

What happened to her, then? I shivered against the rain, silently praying there wasn't an unmarked grave on the property that held her mutilated body. I wanted her to have lived.

The plank still lay at the foot of the mausoleum. I stepped up to it, feeling as though I should put it back in place, but I was reluctant to repeat my experience from the previous day. I walked over the plank instead and pressed my ear to the mausoleum's doors. The wet stone was ice cold against my cheek.

90

This is ridiculous, I thought as I listened to the granite. *What are you hoping for?*

But my heart gave a horrified flutter when I heard a quiet, muffled shuffling noise—footsteps moving closer, dragging on the floor in a way that set my teeth on edge. Fear flared up in my chest, and I didn't dare move as whatever was in the tomb came closer to me, close enough to touch if the door hadn't been in place—

I jerked back as something large pounded on the door. The stone shuddered under the impact, sending vibrations through where my fingers touched it. I stumbled away from it, tripping over the heavy wooden beam as the thing inside the tomb pounded on the door, demanding to be let out...

I ran.

My feet skidded in the mud as I hauled myself through the cemetery, no longer concerned about whether I was stepping on graves. The booming chased me through the gate and across the yard. My stitch flared up, and I couldn't drag air in fast enough to feed my stressed muscles. My throat felt raw, and I realized I'd been screaming.

My legs were shaking and weak. They slipped out from under me as I tried to run up the front porch stairs, and I caught myself on one of the stone pillars. As I hung there, gripping the granite with aching fingers and trying to see through terror-blinded eyes, the booming finally ceased.

I dropped to my knees and fought to keep myself collected. There was something in the mausoleum—something that shouldn't have been alive. And it wanted out.

I thanked my lucky stars that the doors had been locked, not just barred by the wood. Then I prayed that whatever was inside the tomb had no way of unlocking them.

My legs were shaking less, so I pulled myself up, staggered through the house's front door, and pressed it closed behind me. The lock was a useless, flimsy thing that a good kick could have probably broken, but I turned it anyway, and it gave me a very small amount of relief. At least if the thing in the tomb got out, it couldn't enter the house silently.

I sat on the floor for a long time, counting my breaths, waiting for the stitch to subside, and wishing I could call a taxi to take me away from the house that very moment. Instead, I reached into my pocket, pulled out my phone, and dialed Mrs. Gillespie's number. The call went to voicemail.

My brain felt empty as I tried to mumble an explanation. "There's…um…there's a problem. It's…well…I…call me back. Please."

I ended the call with a flick of my thumb then leaned back against the door, resting my head against the cool wood and closing my eyes. Flashing lights danced against the black of my eyelids, as though I'd been staring into a fire, and I was vaguely aware that if I needed to call the police or even an ambulance, it would be over an hour before they reached me. A lot of things could happen in an hour.

Can't stay here for the rest of your life. I set to the job of collecting my aching legs under myself and staggering up the stairs. Mud was smeared halfway up my legs, and dirt clung underneath my fingernails. Another shower was in order, but between the shower earlier that afternoon and spending so long in the rain, I felt like a drowning rat as I stood under the hot stream of water.

What happened out there?

There was something in the crypt; that much was clear. It was strong enough to bow solid granite doors and aware enough to sense me when I approached it. My mind tried, and failed, to connect those two snippets of fact to any sort of logic. My instincts had their own opinion about what lay sleepless in the stone tomb: Jonathan Gillespie.

It's been two hundred years since Jonathan walked on earth, Elle.

I was simply too tired to think any further. Whatever was in the tomb hadn't followed me to the house, so I pushed aside that thought as I cobbled together a dinner. There was hardly any food left; I would need to get into town if I wanted to stay more than another day.

Once I'd finished and washed up, I walked through the house to turn the lights off. It was a little after six in the evening, but it felt much later. The thick rain continued to beat on the house, and the clouds blocked the sunlight as effectively as any blanket could.

As I turned out the lights, I checked the rattraps and poison I'd left. The ones in the kitchen, library, and laundry were untouched. I snorted in frustration and walked past the door that led to the basement. I'd placed traps down there, too, but no way in hell was I going to check them. Mrs. Gillespie could do that herself when she got back.

I climbed the stairs, running one hand along the banister, and walked down the long hallway to my room. The air was colder on the second level, so I pulled more blankets out of the closet and threw them over the bed. Then, on an impulse, I grabbed one corner and began dragging the bed until I'd turned it and moved it against the opposite wall, to where I'd seen Genevieve's bed in my dreams. I crawled under the blankets, lay on my back, and waited for sleep to claim me.

CHAPTER 12
(FOUR)

THERE WAS A HORRIBLE ringing noise in my ears.

Genevieve lay on her side in the small wooden bed, her heavy eyes wide as she clutched her pillow against her chest. I turned and saw her sister sitting up in bed, her knees tucked under her chin. The girl's limp black hair made a curtain around her face as she rocked backward and forward.

"It's been five days," Genevieve whispered. Her lips were pale, and the fierce resolve I'd seen in her before had drained away, leaving a scared child in its place. "Why won't he die?"

The sister didn't answer, and that's when I realized my ears weren't ringing—someone was screaming. I walked to the window and gazed out into the pitch-black night as the three of us listened to Jonathan Gillespie shriek in horror and fury, trapped in the tomb he'd built himself, the tomb Genevieve had locked him in, the tomb where he should have died.

CHAPTER 13
FOURTH NIGHT

I WOKE TO FIND the terrible screaming noise still echoing through the house. For a moment, I thought Jonathan had woken again to wail his fury at the night sky, but I stopped to draw breath and realized the sound had been coming from my own mouth.

The echoes died away as I lay in bed and listened to the house's breathing. It seemed louder than it had been before, as though the house had run a marathon and was dragging in deep, long breaths, rather than the gentle whispers it normally did. Every pipe in the building was alive; every strained wooden brace groaned. The air felt dense, like I'd walked under a power line— and the scratching had returned. It was louder than I'd ever heard it. More insistent.

I got up, wrapping the blanket about my chilled body, and stepped toward where the noise came from the opposite wall. I held my breath and listened as the noise seemed to take on a new timbre.

That's not rats, I realized with a burst of horror. *It's fingernails scratching at wood.*

My feet carried me closer, moving me against my will, until I stood directly in front of the wall. I inhaled deeply, closed my eyes, and pressed my ear to the peeling wallpaper. The scratching noise came through my ears and permeated my body. It was frantic. In the midst of it, I thought I could hear faint gasps.

It was coming from Hanna's room. I stepped back from the wall and pressed my palms into my eyes while I tried to think.

There was something in the house. I was certain of it. It might not have been alive anymore, but whatever—or whoever—it was had refused to move on. I knew what I had to do, and every atom of my body recoiled at the idea.

I pulled my robe on over my pajamas, slipped my feet into my boots, picked the candlestick off the bedside table, and left my bedroom. The door to Hanna's room was still open a fraction, letting a sliver of natural moonlight into the hallway. I approached it slowly, keeping my breathing quiet, and pushed it open.

The room hadn't changed since the day before, but somehow, it looked completely different. The boxes stacked in the middle of the room cast long shadows across the floor. The curtains that had been pastel pink in the daytime looked gray in the moonlight as they shifted slowly in the air current caused by the opening door. The toys in the corner watched me with their beady plastic eyes.

The floorboards creaked under my feet as I stepped fully into the room and looked around for the source of the noise. It came from the wall to the right—the wall that divided this room from my room.

I frowned at it. *Has the noise been coming from my own room after all?*

It couldn't have been. That meant…*it's coming from* inside *the wall.* I stepped back to get a better look at it. The pink floral wallpaper was more modern and in better repair than what covered the rest of the house. I couldn't see any marks in it. The only unique part of the wall was the large wooden wardrobe.

The wardrobe looked as if it might have been from the house's original furnishings. It stood taller than my head, and detailed swirls and strange shapes had been carved into its double doors. I grabbed the handles and pulled the doors open, exposing a cavernous, empty interior.

The scratching persisted, seemingly coming from just behind the wood. I stepped into the wardrobe and pressed my ear to its back. I braced myself by placing my hands on the wood, and I jumped back immediately. A breeze, thin and ice cold, had grazed the fingers of my left hand.

I felt along the back of the cupboard until I found it: about halfway along was a gap in the wood—not large enough to see through to the other side, but wide enough to let a narrow burst of cold air through. I tucked the candlestick into my pocket and began following the crack. It traveled the height of the wardrobe and stopped a half inch above the base. I knelt and felt around it. The crack traveled vertically along the floor before turning upward again to meet the top of the wooden box.

A door?

I tried to get a grip in the crack and pull it open, but neither side budged. It was only when I knelt again and pulled at the base that it began to shift. It was jammed in place by age and neglect, but I managed to get my fingernails under the board and drag it out with a scrape. It was hinged at the top, but the bottom swung up. *Like a human-size cat door.*

I raised it above my head to see the wall behind. The floral wallpaper continued, but a sparkle of gold off to one side caught my eye. I rested the wooden plank on my shoulder as I pulled my cell phone out and shone its light at the glittering object.

It was a tiny key sitting in a keyhole. I reached out to touch the cool metal then, unable to resist the temptation, turned it. It gave a quiet click, followed by a louder grinding noise, and the entire section of the wall pulled away from me, exposing a dark area behind it.

I stood inside the wardrobe for a moment, stunned, then I stepped into the gap. Only about two feet wide, it continued to my right. The weak light of my phone revealed a few stone steps.

"Wow." The scratching hadn't been coming from inside the walls after all; there was an entire passageway *between* them.

It was the early hours of the morning, but that didn't stop me from pulling out my cell phone and calling Mrs. Gillespie. Just like earlier, the call went to voicemail. I didn't bother leaving a message.

I should wait until morning and call again. She needs to know about this.

The hallway stretched before me, tempting me, offering to

solve the puzzles that had plagued me for the previous four days, but I knew it would be insanity to continue down there alone. Intending to step back into Hanna's room, I turned toward the door, just in time to see the last crack of light disappear as the stone door ground into place.

I swore, lunged for the door handle, and tried to pull it back open, but the lock clicked a second before I could find a grip. My fingers shook as I tugged at the door's handle, but it had already sealed itself…and the key was on the other side.

"Damn, damn, damn." I fumbled for my phone. The thin light illuminated my narrow container as I began dialing the emergency help line.

Or I would have dialed them, if my phone's reception hadn't dropped off. *What? But I made a call just a moment ago!*

I stared at the empty corner of the screen where my reception bars should have been, but it stayed stubbornly empty.

It had to be the room, I realized. Being so rural, the Gillespies' house had always had poor reception, but it had never gone below one bar before. Something in that cramped passageway was stopping me from making calls. Maybe the stone walls were lined with something my signal couldn't get through, or maybe it was simply too thick to penetrate. Either way, I was segregated from the outside world, my entry blocked, and only one way to go.

I swore again, this time with feeling.

The stairwell stretched in front of me, dripping with the darkness that permeated the rest of the building. My phone's light wasn't strong enough to penetrate more than two steps ahead. I'd thought the rest of the building was dingy, but the passageway was unnaturally black, almost as if the shadows congregated here.

If the building were alive, this would be its major artery...and the shadows would be its blood.

The scratching had stopped, and I wasn't sure if that was better or worse. The quiet surrounded me, smothering me and stripping away my security. Standing still in the cramped little hallway wasn't going to help me, but taking that first stair down the passageway was one of the hardest things I'd ever done.

Once I'd started, though, I quickly picked up the pace, my boots slapping on the stone ground and my breath deepening. The stairs were steep and narrow, making me feel poised on the edge of toppling into the black abyss, but I didn't dare slow down.

I glanced at the smooth ceiling and tried to work out where I was. The stairs must have been taking me under the second floor's hallway. I remembered how, two days before, I'd been startled by the sound below my feet, but hadn't been able to find anyone in the house. Was this where it had been coming from?

I glanced back down and instantly regretted my distraction as my foot plunged into an empty space where the next step should have been. My hands shot out and grasped at the walls, which were rough and unexpectedly cold under my fingers. For a second, I thought I might be able to regain my balance and pull back, but my momentum had been too strong. I tumbled over the edge in a mess of limbs as I tried to grab on to anything that would break my fall into the inky blackness below.

CHAPTER 14
(FIVE)

THE SHOVEL'S BLADE DUG into the compacted dirt as Genevieve's boot pushed down on it. She was sweating but apparently still didn't dare to shed her heavy black dress—or maybe she didn't have anything to change into.

Her brother with the missing fingers was opposite her, cutting into the ground with his own shovel. They were both panting, although the day was cool and overcast. I looked away from the hole they were carving and saw they were in the cemetery. It had fewer weeds, and the gravestones were clean and new, but in other ways, it was almost identical to the burial ground I'd walked through.

Behind us were three other family members. Genevieve's older sister, the one who shared her bedroom, had tears running down her pale cheeks. She was holding hands with a boy who looked about six and a girl who couldn't have been older than four. In front of them was a long shape wrapped in a white cloth.

The body, waiting for its burial.

The older boy stopped his digging for a moment, his brow creased. "Maria should be the last one, shouldn't she? The darkness won't claim any of us?"

Genevieve's heavy lids fluttered as she glanced over her four remaining relatives. Her eyes were dry, but something dark lingered there. *Guilt,* I thought, *or possibly anger.* "I think so," she said. "He needed us to believe him with our whole hearts to have any power over us. We didn't, so the sickness shouldn't be able to touch us."

"Damn him," the older sister said, but there was no fight left in her voice. "I hope he burns in hell for this, the bastard."

The other two glanced at the mausoleum for barely a second then returned to digging. I walked around them to where a gravestone lay flat on the dirt. It looked bright and clean, ready to be placed as a permanent marker of Maria Gillespie's last bed.

A boom shattered the silence. I jolted backward and stared at the mausoleum; little bits of dirt rained off its roof after something large and fierce had pounded on the doors. The heavy wooden plank was in its brackets, providing a small measure of protection for those outside the tomb.

Genevieve and her siblings stared at the mausoleum for a moment. When there was no more activity, they returned to their chore. I had the impression that wasn't the first time it had happened, and they had made a silent agreement not to speak about it.

I moved away from the mausoleum to stand next to the older sister and the two children. The three watched the cloth-covered body in front of them with an odd mixture of resignation and revulsion. I watched it, too, wondering which one Maria had been, whether I would have recognized her, and what sort of fate had befallen her.

A gust of wind picked up the corner of the cloth and pulled it back from the corpse's face. I recognized one of the middle-aged women—Jonathan's wife, I thought—her eyes open and glassy, her jaw slack, her face as white as the sheets surrounding her. Ugly boils surrounded her jaw and nose, and cracks spread out from her mouth and eyes where the skin had split horribly. Tracks of congealed blood gathered in the splits, looking like dark-red worms crawling across her face.

The older sister moaned and gathered the children to her, burying their faces in her dress so they wouldn't see what had become of the woman they had probably called mother. Genevieve stepped out of the grave. She glanced down at the grisly body for a moment before kicking the cloth back into place.

"Take them inside," she told her sister. Her voice was low and gentle as she brushed a hand over the young girl's head. "You've paid your respects. Paul and I will finish burying her."

I gasped and moaned, rolling to my side as pain flared through my body. My head thundered, my left arm ached, and my back burned. I thought I was going to be sick, but I coiled in on myself on the cold stone ground. Gradually, the pains subsided.

Half of me wished I could have stayed in that dream state

longer; I'd been comfortable there, free from pain and fear. *At least the fall didn't put me into a coma...or worse.*

I sat up and groaned as the headache flared. My phone, which lay facedown, gave off a small amount of light; I grabbed at it before it could power off completely and leave me blind. The screen was cracked, but it was still working.

Behind me was the drop off I'd fallen over—it must have been at least eight feet high—and a collection of white rocks and dark scraps of cloth on the ground. I was incredibly lucky not to have been hurt worse by the fall. The pain was intense, but my limbs all seemed to work, and I didn't think anything vital was broken.

Small gray rocks jutted out of one side of the vertical wall, zigzagging neatly to the floor. *Steps*, I thought, so that the owner of the passageway could climb down easily. The drop off was likely a deliberate trap. For anyone who didn't know the stairs ended, it was all too easy to tumble over the edge and break a leg or a skull on the stone floor.

It took me a few minutes to get to my feet. I was dizzy and aching, but I preferred to deal with the pain rather than spend more time than I had to in the tunnel. I started walking again, still using my damaged phone as a light, but I moved more cautiously, paying greater attention to the ground in front of me in case there was a second trap.

As I moved farther through the tunnel, I thought I saw a hint of light in the distance. Twenty paces on, I was walking down a second flight of stairs, moving quickly again, desperate to reach the golden glow cutting through the dark.

The stairs turned a corner, and I found myself facing a sliver of light barely half an inch wide going from the floor to the tunnel's ceiling.

A door?

I pushed on the walls, but they didn't budge. My hands scrabbled over the smooth surface, searching for any sort of indent or crevice I could get a grip on, but the crack of light in the corner was the only thing breaking up the monotony of the rough stone. Frustrated, I put my cheek against the wall and looked through the gap.

On the other side were…*bookcases?* I gasped, realizing where I was, and felt my heart rate pick up. It was the hidden room with no door I'd found in the library. I was looking through the gap I'd seen the eye in.

Nausea roiled in my stomach as I drew back. I turned in a circle, examining the area behind me. To my left was the staircase I'd just come down. To the right was another turn in the wall and a staircase leading downward again. The wall directly in front of me bore the strange splotch of color that had tricked me into thinking I'd seen someone in the tunnel.

Was it a trick, though? I thought of the scratching noises that had come from the passageway, and the hairs on my arms rose.

There was no way to escape back into the library—I'd tried everything I could think of to get inside on my second night in the building—so I had no choice but to keep moving forward, following the stairwell that led me deeper under the Gillespies' house.

The air was icy cold on my bare arms. My footsteps were

echoing off the stone floor and walls, tricking my ears into imagining a dozen invisible people were following my every movement. It became colder the lower I went, and by the time I thought I had to be equal with the basement, or perhaps even a little lower, my breaths were pluming in front of my face.

The stairwell finally flattened into a long, straight walkway. The gray stone surrounded me, rising above my head in a curved ceiling. I held my light up to the all-consuming darkness, but I couldn't see how far it went. I wanted to stop and rest for a few moments, but the idea of staying in the one spot for too long made my skin crawl. So I kept moving, following the narrow walkway as it carried me toward goodness knew where.

Jonathan Gillespie must have had this constructed at the same time as building the house. For what purpose, though?

I thought back to the article I'd read about the Gillespie cult being run out of a town after a "calamity." Perhaps Jonathan Gillespie had been afraid the townspeople would come after him, so he'd constructed an escape passage. That made sense. I'd been walking for so long that I guessed I had to be outside the house.

In my dream, Genevieve and her remaining family had been burying a horribly mutilated corpse. Genevieve seemed to think Jonathan had caused it and that, because they'd believed Jonathan's teachings, her family had been susceptible to their leader's curse—his revenge, I supposed, for what had been done to him.

It wasn't too hard to imagine the same disease I had seen being the reason his cult had fled from their town on the North Coast. The blog had mentioned that a group of his followers had died in a short span of time. It couldn't have been blatant murder, or Jonathan and his clan would have been arrested straightaway and taken to the gallows. But a disease that had no name or cure and killed in such a grisly way would have caused enough confusion and doubt for Jonathan to usher his remaining loyal followers out of town.

Maria's face rose in my mind, her sheet-white skin split by dozens of dark-red cracks, black blisters pockmarking her cheeks, her blank eyes staring at the sky. "Sicko," I spat.

My pathway, straight and smooth, led me forward for at least forty meters before it ended in a flight of stairs. I jogged up them then finally came to a short landing, where a stone door stood.

This has to be it. With a small surge of relief, I reached for the doorknob. *This will be the exit. It probably leads out somewhere in the woods past the vegetables gardens or—*

"The mausoleum," I gasped in sudden realization. The dread that followed was nearly enough to knock my feet out from under me.

I'd assumed Genevieve had watched her father walk across the grassy lawn behind the building to reach the graveyard. But he hadn't. *Of course* he hadn't. He'd taken the hidden tunnel, his private passageway installed in his own bedroom, and she'd heard his footsteps in the floor below her as she'd lain awake in bed.

I was in the same passageway she'd followed him down that night, relying on the darkness to hide her and the echoes of

Jonathan's footfalls to mask her own steps, as she'd stalked him to his mausoleum and locked him inside.

She'd trapped him using the very same door I was about to open.

"No," I moaned. The word echoed around me, as though the walls were repeating my lament. "Please, please, no."

I wanted to turn around, to leave the hideous tomb unopened, to protect myself from whatever was inside. Even dying alone and cold in the passageway seemed preferable to turning the dark, rusted doorknob in front of me. I made to take a step backward, and a dizzying sensation rolled though me.

My awareness was tugged from my body, as though my soul were being split from my flesh. My stomach dropped, and I gasped, trying not to lose my balance, trying not to lose my *mind*, as physical and mental were torn apart.

Then I was in Genevieve's consciousness.

CHAPTER 15
(SIX)

SHE STOOD IN FRONT of the very same door I was confronting, one hand holding a candle, the other on the doorknob. Her face was only vaguely familiar. Her eyes were still dark and heavy lidded, but her black hair was streaked gray, and loosely wrinkled skin had softened her heavy-jawed face. She still wore all black, but the dress was worlds apart from the plain, ugly affair her father had clothed her in. It was made from rich satins, ruffled at the shoulders and the waist and decorated with black lace and pearls.

I gaped at her, amazed by the change. She had to be at least eighty.

She took a deep, slow breath, and her eyes fluttered closed as she braced herself for what was about to come. Hanging from a silk ribbon tied around her right wrist was a large shard of brilliantly blue crystal shaped like a teardrop and sharpened at one end.

Genevieve let out the breath, opened her eyes, and turned the handle to open the door. She stepped through the opening into the inky blackness beyond, then the thick stone door slammed shut behind her. I heard her voice ring out, firm and fierce, "Hello, Father."

Reentering my body was like jumping off the top of a cliff, but instead of falling, I was sucked up toward the sky. I dropped to my knees, gasping air into my lungs and fighting the need to be sick as my consciousness reconnected with each of my limbs. My brain was one of the last parts to anchor itself, and my vision swam as I blinked in the faint light of my phone.

"What was *that*?" I gasped at the empty hallway. "Genevieve?"

Silence answered me. I let my body roll over, waiting for the unnatural feeling of being disconnected from myself to fade.

Apparently, it was much easier for Genevieve to take over my mind—I was sure that was what had been happening—when I was asleep. I felt as if I'd been hit by a train. My limbs shook as I propped myself against the wall.

I realized that she'd been showing me those snapshots of her life for a reason. There was something she needed me to do, and I wanted to scream at just the thought of it.

Genevieve was the only member of her family who did not have a plot of land in the graveyard. That was because she'd never been buried. She'd gone into Jonathan's crypt to face whatever was left of him…and she'd lost. I knew, with complete certainty, that her bones were lying just behind the door I sat next to, while her spirit wandered the passageway for eternity, seeking someone to complete the impossible, terrible task she'd committed to.

She needed me to kill Jonathan Gillespie.

I shook my head and pressed the palms of my hands against my eyelids, fighting tears. My fingers trembled as I spoke into the darkness. "Please, don't ask me to do this. I can't. I'm not strong enough. You have to find someone else. *Please.*"

An icy hand brushed over my cheek, wiping at the tears there. I jolted back and held up my light to see the hallway, but it was empty.

Heat spread from where I'd been touched. It seeped through my face, drawing blood to my cheeks, and ran down my shoulders. As if a bucket of hot water had been poured over me, the warmth coursed through my chest and into my stomach. From there, it poured into my legs and my arms, right down to my fingers and toes, until every cell of my body felt hot and alive.

Liquid confidence followed the heat, and I drew in a shuddering breath. I was capable, I realized—and I was Genevieve's last hope. She believed I could finish what she'd started. She *trusted* me.

More than that, I felt the urgency of the task. It had been more important than Genevieve's life and was more important than my own. Whatever happened, I had to destroy what remained of the cult leader. I *had* to.

I already had the physical strength, and she'd lent me her mental fortitude. I could sense her smiling at me through the darkness, and I hazarded a smile back.

My aches and bruises forgotten, I pushed myself to my feet and faced the door. I felt vulnerable and empty-handed, but then something invisible guided my fingers to my jean's left pocket. I found the candlestick I'd tucked there before entering the hallway. "Thanks," I said, pulling it free and brandishing it in my left hand, resting my right on the door handle. "Ready?"

Her silent approval urged me on, and I turned the cold knob.

Two centuries was a long time for a door to be neglected, but it ground open under my touch, sending a high squeal of rusty metal echoing through the passageway behind me. As the gap widened, I was washed in a wave of foul, stale air. I gripped my candlestick in my left hand and raised the light in my right as I stepped over the threshold and into the mausoleum.

I could *feel* the darkness. The blackness of the hallway hadn't been my imagination after all; it had been seepage of the concentrated inky shadows of the mausoleum: Jonathan's shrine to a world devoid of light.

The door scraped shut behind me, and a dull thud told me it was sealed. I edged to my left, keeping my back to the wall, and my foot landed on something hard and brittle. I bent down to shine my light at the thing I'd stepped on and recoiled; I'd crushed the skeletal remains of a hand sticking out of a stained, decayed black silk dress.

Genevieve.

I'd been expecting it, but it still made me want to scream. I raised the candlestick and wiped the back of my hand across my eyes, where tears of fear and grief were gathering.

Don't think on it, I sensed Genevieve tell me. *It's not me you need to worry about.*

I nodded, tried to slow my breathing, and raised my light toward the rest of the room. That was when I became aware of a sound directly in front of me. Like bones scraping across stone, as something heavy and large moved closer.

My heart was ready to explode. I kept my lower back pressed against the wall but leaned my torso forward and extended my arm to shine the phone's light as far into the smothering shadows as I could.

Jonathan Gillespie loomed out of the darkness, reaching a long, grasping hand toward my face.

Time had decayed him unnaturally. His skin hadn't decomposed. Instead, it had toughened like leather that puckered and bulged over his bones. His eyes were milky white, but tendrils of black, as though his veins had been filled with ink, wove around the empty eyeballs as they swiveled blindly in their sockets.

He'd either lost or torn off his clothes during his imprisonment in the tomb, and his naked body contorted and moved horribly, as though the muscles had atrophied and the bones had fused and broken in strange places. As I watched, his left hand swung backward, the elbow bending ninety degrees in the wrong direction, before it snapped forward again to grab in my direction.

Even worse, his skin had split just like Maria Gillespie's. Cracks grew out from his lips, his collarbone, his elbows, his stomach, and his groin. They flapped open and closed as he moved, and I thought I could see something writhing and *alive* inside of them.

I screamed and dived backward, tripping over Genevieve's corpse and landing on the ground. Jonathan's neck twisted to turn his head in my direction, followed by his shoulders. Then his back shifted one vertebra at a time, and his body clicked into place like an elongated Rubik's Cube. His mouth opened, and some of the *alive* stuff poured out.

It was blackness in a way I'd never seen it before. It was darker than ink and flowed like liquid metal as it dribbled over his chin and ran down his body in rivulets. Each dribble of darkness sought one of the cracks in his skin, where they burrowed back inside of him like cockroaches hiding from the light.

He was almost on top of me. I thought I heard Genevieve talking to me, but my terror was so great that a harsh ringing filled my ears—I couldn't have understood her words even if I'd heard them. I swung my candlestick at Jonathan's head. It denting the skull under the bloated, pocked skin and cut a new gash in his flesh. More of the liquid shadows poured out, and drops landed on my arm. They instantly began attacking me, squirming over my flesh, trying to dig through my skin and get inside of me.

I screamed in pain, and Genevieve's voice suddenly became clear. *The light! The light!*

My hand moved as if on its own, shining the phone at the black chewing through my skin. The tendrils squirmed and dropped off my skin, hitting the floor with heavy plops and wriggling out of the reach of my light.

The distraction had given Jonathan the precious seconds he'd needed. He was on me before I could move, his body pressing against mine, his decayed fingers gripping at my skin and refusing to let go. I stared into his milky eyes as they rotated wildly in their sockets, as if they were trying to see me through their blindness. One of his hands found my neck. He was strong, stronger even than he had been in life, and his fingers forced my mouth open. He inclined his head toward me as though to kiss me, and his lips parted to let the living black drip into my mouth.

Don't swallow! Genevieve screamed in my head. *Fight!*

I squirmed, writhing under the monster, and freed my right hand. I brought the phone up, pushing it between our faces, shining its light directly into his open maw. Jonathan howled, and the noise was one of the worst sounds I'd ever heard. His grip slackened enough to let me get my other hand free. I cracked the candlestick across his skull a second time, denting its other side.

He recoiled from the impact, and I tried to make a break for it. I managed to wriggle my torso out from under him before his impossibly strong arms locked onto my legs. The grip was so tight I thought he might break my bones. I shone the light at his face again, but his mouth was closed. His skin protected the blackness, and the light didn't affect him. He began to drag himself up my body, pinning me beneath his incredible weight.

The crystal, Genevieve instructed, panic clear in her voice. *Behind you!*

I threw my head back and spotted the shard of blue stone that had been tied around her wrist. It had fallen near the back of the room, just out of my reach.

I began to wriggle, pulling myself toward it an inch at a time. Jonathan was dragging himself up my chest now, and one of his hands shot out and forced the phone from my grip. It fell and skidded out of reach, its weak light barely allowing me to see Jonathan's manic leer as his mouth opened again.

I brought the candlestick across his jaw, but before I could pull my hand back to hit him again, his fingers had tightened around my wrist, immobilizing it.

"No," I moaned, fighting his weight. I looked behind myself for a second and thought I saw the crystal glowing faintly among the shadows, then Jonathan's spare hand gripped my chin again. I threw my free hand backward, grasping at empty ground as Jonathan forced open my lips. My fingers seized on a hot, hard shape, and, praying it was the crystal, I drew it up and slashed at Jonathan's face.

Light, just as alive as the darkness was, sparked where my weapon cut his cheek. Jonathan howled, his eyes rolling maniacally in their sockets, as every fissure in his body spewed out the blackness as if it had been expelled under immense pressure. It writhed across his flesh like a swarm of black worms and began burrowing back into his carcass.

Stab through his skull, Genevieve urged, and I thrust my makeshift dagger upward, toward one of the hideous eyes. It cut through the sack, and more black liquid poured over my hand and ran down my arm as Jonathan's scream rose in pitch. I pushed harder, forcing the blade through the eye socket, into where his brain would have been if he'd still been alive, and suddenly, there was light fizzling and spitting out of the crevices around his eyes and mouth. The corpse thrashed and twitched on top of me as a river of living blackness rushed out of him, drowning me in that tomb of darkness.

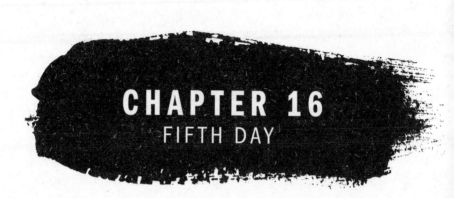

CHAPTER 16
FIFTH DAY

I GASPED, GAGGED, AND spat a mouthful of black gunk onto the floor. It lay there, forming a disgusting puddle but no longer wriggling or moving.

For a moment, I thought I was dead, but as Genevieve's courage wore off, the aches and pains of the last few days returned to me, telling me that I was very much alive.

Jonathan's corpse lay on top of me, immobile. He was much lighter than he had been before, like a sponge after its water had been wrung out, and even though my limbs felt like putty, I was able to push him off. The corpse flopped to the ground, and I scrambled back, gasping and unable to control my shaking.

A long time passed before I felt in control enough to pick up my phone, which had gained another large crack but was amazingly still functioning, and examine the mausoleum.

The claustrophobic blackness had abated. The space was still dark, but my phone's light could penetrate to the opposite wall.

Jonathan's corpse had crumpled on the floor like a rag doll. The luminosity of his paper-white skin looked alien. The shard of crystal poked out of his eye socket, and a small trickle of black sludge dripped off its end.

There wasn't much else to see. A raised dais stood in the center. It had probably served as Jonathan's table while he was alive and his bed during his long years of imprisonment. At one end was a familiar shape: the Book of the Others. The rest of the slate-gray room was empty.

"What now, Genevieve?" I waited expectantly, but the little voice in my head had gone quiet. I turned in a semicircle to look at her skeleton, stupidly expecting it to open its jaw and tell me what to do, but no matter how alive Genevieve's spirit was, her body was long dead.

A hint of silver around the skeleton's neck attracted my attention. I stepped up to it gingerly, muttering apologies under my breath as I pulled a necklace from under the decayed silk dress. On the end of it was a key.

"This will work, right?"

Again, I received no answer. I had the feeling Genevieve had lost the power to talk to me when the energy of the room, whatever had been animating that black stuff, was destroyed. *Maybe she's finally been able to move on? Wish I could have said goodbye.*

I stumbled to the front of the mausoleum, where the two heavy stone doors separated me from the graveyard. After a moment of searching with my phone's light, I found the keyhole, which the key fit without much resistance.

I'm lucky I never put the plank back in place, I thought as I put my shoulder against the door and pushed with the last of my strength. It grated outward slowly, laboriously, and a crack of early-morning sunlight hit my face. *Guess I can thank procrastination for getting me out of here.*

I laughed; I couldn't stop myself. The combined relief of my escape, the joy at seeing real, honest natural light, and the shock of what had just happened overwhelmed me. As I squeezed through the gap in the doors and collapsed in the middle of the graveyard, I let the emotions overtake me, alternatively laughing, crying, and heaving huge, dizzying breaths of clean air.

I propped myself up against Maria Gillespie's gravestone and dialed the number on the small scrap of paper I still had in my pocket. I half expected to go through to voicemail again, but Mrs. Gillespie answered on the fourth ring, sounding exasperated. "What is it now?"

Her curt tone didn't bother me. After meeting Jonathan Gillespie, it was almost a relief to talk to someone so incredibly harmless.

I hadn't decided how much of that night I should tell her about. I supposed it would probably come down to how much of it I thought she would believe...and I suspected that was very little. But there was one thing I thought she should know, as soon as possible, and before I told anyone else.

When I'd fallen off the drop off in the passageway, I'd noticed clumps of old fabric and white rocks on the ground. Once my head had cleared, I'd begun to suspect they weren't rocks at all, but something very valuable I'd crushed during my fall.

I didn't feel like small talk, and I knew Mrs. Gillespie wouldn't tolerate it even if I tried, so I got straight to the point. "I think I found your daughter."

Her sharp inhale told me I'd finally gotten her attention.

The police had thought Hanna died in the vast forest behind the house. Mrs. Gillespie had believed her daughter was kidnapped. Both were wrong.

Without being able to ask either of the people involved, I could only guess at what had actually happened. After Genevieve lost her final fight against her father, her ghost—or spirit or whatever had let her interact with the human world—had lingered in the passageway between the crypt and the house, seeking help to finish the undead monster in the mausoleum.

Hanna had been the first to hear her, though. Without realizing she was talking to a child, Genevieve had called for help. And without realizing she was far too young for the task, Hanna had answered. She'd discovered the flap behind her wardrobe, found the key for it, and entered the tunnel. Of course, Jonathan Gillespie's trap had claimed her life before she'd even left the boundaries of the house.

CHAPTER 17
SILENCE

HANNA'S FUNERAL WAS A very quiet one. Mrs. and Mr. Gillespie stood by the graveside, next to the priest, and watched as the child's coffin was lowered into the ground. Two of their good friends—I think their names were Mallory—hovered a little behind them, and I stood still farther off, feeling like an intruder watching a very personal moment.

The Gillespies' eyes were dry. I had the feeling they'd exhausted all of their grief during the years they'd spent searching for their daughter. This end, while sad, seemed also somehow very comforting to them.

It was a gorgeous warm day, and the cemetery the Gillespies had chosen, the town's public cemetery rather than the little patch behind their house, was filled with trees, flowering bushes, and insects.

I'd been staying at a hotel in the town while the police scoured the hidden passageways and mausoleum. Normally, I wouldn't have been able to afford the room for so long, but according to Mrs. Gillespie's lawyer, the reward Mrs. Gillespie had offered for information that led to Hanna's discovery was mine. I'd made an effort to reject it, but the lawyer had said Mrs. Gillespie was adamant that I should have it.

It was a week after my night in the mausoleum, and the police investigation was wrapping up. Because Jonathan Gillespie's corpse couldn't be identified, he was given a pauper's grave in the town's cemetery. Genevieve had been interred with the rest of her family behind the house.

The priest said a final few words that I couldn't catch, and Mrs. Gillespie nodded curtly then turned to speak with her friends. I loitered for a couple of minutes, unsure of whether I was supposed to stay or leave quietly, but as soon as I turned to go, I heard Mrs. Gillespie's voice ring out, "Just a moment, Elle."

I waited while she said goodbye to the Mallorys and approached me. She was wearing a navy business suit and looked incredibly out of place in the relaxed, parklike graveyard.

"I realized this morning I hadn't thanked you properly." Her voice was much softer than I'd ever heard it. I wondered if this was how she spoke when she wasn't feeling pressured.

"Don't worry about it," I said "I'm—I'm sorry about... everything."

She waved away my lame apology. "Don't be. It's been a long time since I last had hope that I would find my daughter alive. At least this way, I have some closure."

"Yeah," I mumbled, scuffing my shoes through the grass. One question had been weighing on me, but I didn't know how to ask it without seeming rude. "So, uh, your retreat's been cut short. I guess you'll be moving back home now."

Mrs. Gillespie laughed. It was such an unexpected sound that I startled.

"No, no, we're not moving back there. We only stayed because…well, I suppose it was always a stupid dream, but I kept imagining I might open the front door one day and find Hanna on the other side. We moved into the house because of her, and we stayed there because of her. Now that…" She gestured toward the burial plot, and I nodded. "Now that it's over, Mark and I will be moving back to the city. It suits us much better, and I'll be able to rejoin my old law firm."

I did a double-take. "You're…?"

She quirked an eyebrow at me, but a faint smile was playing about her mouth. "I'm a lawyer. Didn't you know that?"

The office at the back of the house flashed through my mind, and I suddenly felt foolish for assuming it belonged to Mr. Gillespie.

"Sorry," I said, but Mrs. Gillespie laughed again.

"Don't worry about it."

Silence lapsed over us for a moment. Mrs. Gillespie's gaze had returned to the plot where her daughter lay. Her expression was soft and a little sad, and once again, I felt as if I were imposing on a personal moment. I desperately dug around for something to break the silence.

"I guess being in law will come in handy for selling the house," I said at last. Mrs. Gillespie turned back to me, and I could see in her face that she hadn't heard me fully. "You'll be able to draft your own legal documents."

"Oh." Understanding flashed over her face, and she smiled again, though she was starting to look tired. "No, we're not selling the house. It's been passed down through the family from my great-great-grandmother, who helped build it. I never liked the place, but it's something I want to keep for when my nephews and nieces are old enough to live on their own. If they want it, anyway."

It was the second curve ball of the morning. I stared at Mrs. Gillespie. Now that I was paying attention, I realized her streaky gray hair would have probably been midnight black at one time, and her jaw, while still feminine, had a hint of thickness to it. "You're a Gillespie? I thought Mr. Gillespie—"

Both of her eyebrows shot up at that. "My husband's name is Mr. Hammond. I had a very strong career when I married Mark, and it made sense to keep my maiden name."

"Wow," I muttered. Now that I knew what to look for, it was obvious that Mrs. Gillespie was only a few generations away from Genevieve. They even had the same fiery look hidden in their cool eyes. I could only imagine how terrifying she was when she was defending a client in court. "I shouldn't have assumed."

She waved away my apology again. "Don't mind it."

"So the house will be left empty?" I asked.

She nodded. "I guess it will. I couldn't sell it, and I don't know how many people would be interested in renting such a rural property…especially with its history." She quirked a smile at me. "Unless you want it?"

She'd asked as a joke, I knew, but as we stared at each other in lengthening silence, we both realized what my answer would be.

"*Do* you want it?" she asked, a little incredulous.

I thought of the house—with the shadowy hallways, the beautiful woods just behind it, the way it seemed to go on forever, and how it breathed late at night—and nodded. "Could I? Would you mind? I wouldn't own it—you can keep it in the family. I could just stay there for a while and keep an eye on it. Like an extended housesitting session."

She looked surprised. Her eyes darted across my face, as if testing to see if I was being serious, and my pleading look must have been enough of an answer for her. "Well, okay then."

"Yes?"

"Yes. I'll have to run it by Mark, but I don't think he'll mind." The gentle smile flickered over her face again. "If you really want it…yes, I think that might work out well for all of us."

It's been six weeks since I officially moved into the Gillespie house. I've spent a lot of my time bringing the furniture down from storage and making the building feel like a home.

The chandelier in the dining room doesn't look out of place anymore now that the ancient, chipped mahogany table is set up below it. The library isn't full, but at least it's no longer empty. I found boxes upon boxes of books in storage and added my own collection to the mix.

The garden beds out back are repaired and filled with compost and seeds. The first shoots are starting to come up. I planted a lot of tomatoes as a tribute to Hanna. Apparently, they were her favorite plant.

The reward money has been an incredible gift. It not only let me break the lease of my old apartment early, but if I manage it carefully and supplement my food shopping with vegetables from the garden, it should keep me going for quite a few years.

That's more than enough time to have a good, solid shot at something that used to just be a dream: publishing my own novel. I've nearly finished a first draft, and I have a folder full of plot notes for a sequel. I have no idea if anything will come from it, but things feel *right* like they never have before. I'm cautiously hopeful.

Genevieve visited my dreams for the first few nights after I moved in. She was a lot weaker than when the living blackness in the mausoleum had been feeding her energy, and she couldn't place me inside her memories anymore. Instead, she showed them to me, like a movie. She wanted me to know that, despite a horrible beginning and terrible end, she had lived a happy life.

After the plague wiped out most of the family, Genevieve and her four siblings struggled to find their place in the world for the first few months. Her older brother, the one missing three fingers, had a good mind for business, and within four years, he owned his own company in town. He married a sweet girl, who'd come to live at Gillespie House. Steve, the man who wrote the blog I'd found, is her grandson.

Over four decades, the Gillespies built their company into an industry, and they became one of the wealthiest families in town. Although both of her younger siblings had married, Genevieve and her older sister never did, but their burgeoning collection of nieces, nephews, and eventually grand-nieces and grand-nephews, meant the house never felt empty.

Genevieve was eighty-six when she found an obscure book talking about the black magic her father had wielded and how tanzanite, the crystal she'd fashioned into a dagger, could be used against it. Her siblings had put the mausoleum out of mind and steered their children away from the graveyard, but Genevieve had never forgotten about how her trapped father had screamed until his vocal cords were shredded or how he had banged on the door anytime she disturbed his rest.

She hadn't told anyone of her plans, and when she didn't come down for breakfast one morning and an exhaustive search failed, no one had thought to look in the hidden passageway that was almost completely forgotten.

The house had stayed in the family for generations. Out of tradition, Jonathan Gillespie's room was never occupied…until, of course, Hanna had taken a liking to the bay window. Genevieve's activity had been accepted as normal house noises. When she slammed the hidden door, people complained about how drafty the house was. When she walked through the passageway, they assumed another of the house's occupants was moving about. When she scratched at the walls, they thought they had rats.

She could finally rest, though, she told me during the last night she shared my dreams. She thanked me for what I'd done and told me she was happy I was enjoying her family's home.

When I woke up the next morning, the house felt slightly different, as though a long-term occupant had moved out. I miss Genevieve, but I'm glad she's finally at peace.

I found the painting of her. It was the last one behind the stack of oil portraits I'd found in the upstairs room. Her dark hair was streaking with gray, a lot like Mrs. Gillespie's, and her face had grown many wrinkles, most of them around her mouth after an abundance of smiles. It must have been painted not long before her final visit to Jonathan; the tanzanite jewel that she'd used to fight her father sparkled beautifully on her necklace. I hung her painting in the middle of the hallway, between the paintings of the rest of her family, so she can continue to watch over the rooms.

The house is beautiful. It's all I ever wanted in a home. Mrs. Gillespie seems happy to have someone to maintain the building until it's reclaimed by another of the Gillespie descendants, and I'm happy to stay as long as she will let me. I feel like a fuller, happier person here. Every morning, I wake up to a sense of excitement and anticipation, and every night, I go to sleep to the sounds of the house breathing around me.

BED AND BREAKFAST

RORY DROPPED HER SUITCASE on the weed-choked earth and slammed her car trunk closed. Finding Mistral Bed and Breakfast had taken longer than she'd expected, and the sun was already creeping behind the gnarled pine trees at the back of the property.

It looks the part, at least. Rory took the small digital camera out of her pocket, leaned against the side of her worn-down car, and snapped a photo. Half the hotels she stayed at were too modern and sterilized to have any sort of atmosphere; the other half were just plain depressing. Mistral, though, could have fallen out of a horror film. Streaks of dying light sliced over the cracked stone house at the center of the property. Two stories of bedrooms extended from both sides of the main building. Their off-white paint had come away in huge flakes, and one of the rooms was missing its door.

It's strange that there weren't any photos of this place online. Maybe no one else could find it. Although its lane had speared off a main freeway, the B&B didn't have any signage to attract guests, and the building wasn't visible from the road. Rory had assumed the lane led to a private property the first three times she'd driven past it.

"Want a room?"

The voice was alarmingly close, and Rory sucked in a breath as she turned. A woman, bone-thin and wearing a faded ankle-length yellow dress, stood in the clearing. She held something silvery in her hand, and a stab of shock hit Rory as she recognized a cleaver.

"Rooms are fifty a night. Breakfast included." The woman's sunken eyes didn't blink as they stared at Rory, but her voice was sharp and quick.

If she hadn't promised her blog readers that she would spend the night in Mistral Bed and Breakfast, Rory would have been sorely tempted to slink back into her car and endure the four-hour drive back to her home. Instead, she fixed a wide smile on her face and said, "Sounds great. Book me in."

"This way." The woman turned toward the main building, and Rory caught sight of a limp, bloodied shape held in the woman's other hand.

It took her a second to recognize it as a decapitated chicken. *She must have a farm behind the house. It's a long drive to the nearest shopping center, so she probably tries to be self-sufficient. Come to think of it, it's a long drive to anywhere.*

Rory cleared her throat as they climbed the porch leading to the stone house. "I had some trouble finding the right turnoff."

"Most people do." The woman held the door open just long

enough for Rory to duck through, then she discarded the dead chicken and the bloodied hatchet into a bucket by the doorstop.

Inside, the house was oppressively dim. Rory could make out the outline of a grandfather clock and a large dark-wood desk. She waited for her hostess to turn on the lights, but the woman didn't. Instead, she rounded the desk, pulled out a guest book, and shoved it toward Rory. "Name, address, phone number. How many nights?"

"Just the one." Rory scribbled her details, then glanced further up the page. The most recent guest was from three months before. In fact, an entire year's worth of visitors fit onto a single page. "Ah…business is a bit quiet, isn't it?"

The woman simply drew the book out from under Rory's hands and slammed it closed. "We get by. Do you want a downstairs room?"

Rory glanced toward the windows. Thin white curtains didn't help the room's starvation of light, but a glimpse of her car and its boxes of equipment was comforting. "Actually, I'm here because I run a ghost research blog. One of my readers requested I visit. Have you noticed a presence or supernatural phenomenon in any of your rooms?"

The woman didn't speak for a long time. Her cold, sunken eyes stared without blinking from behind stray strands of gray hair, but Rory thought she saw the woman's lips pull more tightly together, as though she'd scented something unpleasant.

"There are no ghosts here," she said at last, and her voice was definitely tighter than it had been before.

Rory gave a quick nod of acceptance. "That's okay. Put me in the room with the best view, then."

Her host didn't speak or move. Rory was starting to worry she'd inadvertently insulted her—not every hotel owner liked the idea of being on a ghost hunting blog—and quickly pulled her wallet out of her jacket pocket. "It was fifty for the night, wasn't it?"

"And breakfast." The woman's lips twisted as she took the cash, but her tone had returned to its even, emotionless cadence. "Room eight. Follow me."

She snagged a key off a dusty key ring behind the desk then led Rory back out the front door. The sun had almost entirely disappeared behind the horizon, leaving the wooded landscape in a surreal state of twilight. Rory grabbed her suitcase from beside the car and followed the hotel owner up an external flight of stairs to the second-floor rooms, then to the farthest room along—the one at the end of the block.

"Breakfast is between seven and nine." The woman's eyes fixed on Rory, forceful and insistent. "Checkout is by ten. I'll knock on your door to let you know when it's bedtime; once you hear my knock, don't leave your room until sunrise."

Rory had reached out to take the key but stopped at the last statement. Her face didn't know whether to form a smile or a frown and awkwardly managed both at once. "Sorry, was that a jo—"

"Don't cause trouble." The thin woman thrust the key into Rory's hand then clattered down the stairs. Rory watched her until she disappeared into the main building, then exhaled heavily and turned to unlock her door.

I've stayed in a lot of dodgy hotels since I started this blog. There was that place in Carthage that had cockroaches coming out of the taps. When the heater in the Moors Point B&B broke, I thought I might actually freeze to death. And there's no forgetting the multiple used condoms I found in that sleazy Kettletree place. But this may just be my first ever one-star hotel.

Rory paused, her fingers lingering over her laptop's keyboard. It was a tough choice to know what to write next; should she mention how she was sitting cross-legged on the bed on account of that being the only furniture in the room? Should she describe the dust that coated every surface, the suspicious stain she'd uncovered behind the bed's headboard, or the way the light occasionally flickered before stabilizing with a dull hiss?

The room was small, and it felt even smaller once her equipment was set up. A video camera sat on a tripod in the corner opposite the door. The second, higher-definition motion-detection camera, which Rory would turn on shortly before going to bed, would activate only if it sensed movement in the room. An EMF recorder sat on top of her travel case. Mistral Bed and Breakfast didn't offer any closets, so Rory had resigned herself to wearing crumpled clothes the next day.

The equipment was largely for show. When she returned home,

she would edit the video footage down to a choice couple of minutes: reaction shots of her exploring the poky room then a summary of her experience recorded either during breakfast or in the car drive home. Neither the motion camera nor the EMF recorder had seen much action since she'd bought them two years previously.

Rory made no secrets about her belief in the supernatural—or, rather, her lack of belief. Her shtick was that she was a skeptic rigorously investigating—and debunking—haunted hotels. When she'd started her blog, she'd expected to build a following of like-minded readers. It had been a huge surprise to get fan mail from people who claimed to firmly believe in ghosts.

Rory worked hard to make sure each post was entertaining. She accepted suggestions for hotels she should visit—that was how she'd ended up at dead-end Mistral—and dutifully investigated each location as thoroughly as she could in a single night. It was fun for her, and the readers ate it up. In the time she'd been debunking haunted locations, she'd met the full gamut of hotel owners. Some didn't want their reputation tainted. Others wanted to embrace notoriety and eagerly asked her what she'd found. And one very memorable owner had tried to fake a haunting, complete with sound effects and rattling door handles. That location had produced Rory's most-read post.

A sharp knock on the door startled her, and Rory stood. "Hello?"

"It's bedtime," the strange hotel owner called. "Stay in your room until morning."

Rory turned to the camera and gave it a bemused reaction

shot. She still wasn't sure if the woman was joking or being serious, but she called back, "Okay. Good night, sleep tight."

There was no reply, but a strange, scraping noise came through the thin door. Rory frowned, picked the camera off its tripod, and carried it to near the door so that it would pick up the noise. Wet sticking noises punctuated the scrapes, almost like a paintbrush.

Rory held her breath for a beat as she listened to the noise, then she called, "Hello?"

A dull thud like a wooden object being dropped into a bucket was followed by footsteps moving down the stairwell. Rory waited until she was certain her host had gone, then she opened the door.

"Oh, what the hell?"

Rory glanced over the rail that bordered the stairwell to make sure she was alone, then hurried to change the settings on her camera so that the door would be visible in the pale moonlight.

She panned the camera across the door then stepped forward so that she would be in the shot. "Okay, it's eleven thirty at night, and I just got my 'go to bed' knock. But look what she did to my door before she left. I swear this wasn't here when I checked in."

Rory repositioned the camera to film the door again. A large X had been smeared over the surface, all four corners touching the edges of the frame. It was hard to be sure in the dim light, but the liquid looked red. Rory dabbed a finger on one of the dribbles.

"It's wet," she said, rubbing her finger and thumb together. "Kind of…uh…tacky. Not smooth like paint. Guys, I think this might be blood."

A hysterical laugh built inside her chest, but Rory clamped her lips shut before it could escape. The main building was close, and she didn't want to attract her host's ire.

She slipped back inside her room, returned the camera to its tripod, and moved into the cramped bathroom to wash her hand. The dingy yellow towel hung beside the sink looked dusty, so Rory dried her hands on her jeans as she returned to the main room.

What did I do to earn an X on my door? And if that really was blood, where did she get it from? The memory of the headless chicken answered the *what*, but did little to solve the *why*.

Rory was starting to suspect she'd stumbled into a hoax. If Mistral had so few guests, a desperate owner might try to drum up business any way she could—including faking a haunting. Ghost tours were a surprisingly healthy industry, and Rory knew of more than one hotel that survived on curious thrill-seekers.

An anonymous commenter had left the request to visit Mistral. While the bed-and-breakfast didn't seem to have technology more advanced than a radio—Rory's room didn't even have a TV—it wasn't impossible to imagine the hotel owner using a library's computers to submit the comment or even asking one of her friends to do it for her.

No matter how or why Rory had ended up there, it would all be good fuel for her blog. The house's atmosphere was the perfect level of neglected and unsettling that her readers craved, and the hoax would provide an addictive narrative.

On the flipside, it meant she would probably have to pull an all-nighter to document the experience. Rory sighed, stretched, and pulled a packet of nuts and a bottle of water out of her bag. She was craving caffeine, but her room had no kettle.

I'd be better off if I were camping, she thought ruefully as she chewed on a peanut. *At least then, I could have a fire.*

Rory lifted her head from her laptop and rubbed at her sore eyes. It wasn't long past midnight, and she'd turned the room's light off and dimmed her computer screen to give the impression that she'd gone to sleep. If the hotel owner was planning to fake a haunting, Rory wasn't going to make the job easy.

Something crunched below her window. Rory held her breath and listened; what sounded like footsteps moved through the yard behind her room. Being careful not to make too much noise, Rory rose and crept toward the small window. The long white curtains obstructing her view would also help keep her hidden. She leaned as close to the glass as she dared and peered into the property's backyard.

As she'd suspected, a large vegetable patch and chicken coop took up much of the clearing. Tall trellises cut through the moonlight, creating spikes of black over the ground. A solitary chopping block stood near the building, where an ax protruded from the log. Rory squinted to see the woman, but as far as she could tell, the yard was empty.

She stepped away from the window and was about to return

to her computer when a hard noise stopped her. Breath held, Rory returned to the view of the yard.

A man stood at the chopping block. As Rory watched, he lifted the ax and brought it down in a long arc to cleave a slice of wood in half. He then bent, picked up a fresh log, and put it into position.

How didn't I see him before? Frowning, Rory reached into her pocket for her camera. *Is he the hostess's husband? And why's he chopping wood after midnight? Is this meant to disturb me?*

His back to the window, he brought the ax down in a series of quick arcs to turn the log into kindling. He seemed just as thin and wiry as his wife, and from what Rory could see, his clothes were no less dirty. Rory lifted the camera to her eye, focused it on the figure, waited for him to raise the ax, then snapped a photo.

Light burst across the scene, and Rory swore under her breath as she ducked below the window. She'd forgotten to turn off the flash.

Despite the sharp embarrassment spreading heat across her face, Rory lifted herself to her knees to peer over the windowsill. The ax stood in the chopping block, and the yard was empty. She frowned. *He's disappeared again—but where to? I didn't hear any footsteps.*

As she sank back below the window frame, she clicked the camera's button to retrieve the most recent photo. It was, to her frustration, slightly blurry. Shock had moved Rory's hand too soon, and not much of the figure was clear except for his eyes. He'd somehow sensed her and turned just as the picture was being taken. She could make out a grizzled, twisted face fitted with two bright reflective lights where his eyes should have been.

Rory's mouth was dry. She put the camera aside and went into the bathroom to drink from its sink. *It's not unusual for light to reflect off eyes. You've seen it a hundred times before.*

She splashed water across her face. It was cold enough to sting. She still wasn't desperate enough to use the towel hung beside the sink, so Rory wiped her face on her jacket's sleeve instead. Every time she blinked, she saw the gaunt, sagging face and its flashing-light eyes as though the memory had been seared onto the backs of her eyelids.

"Stop being a baby." Rory stalked into the main room, though she stayed well away from the curtains. "They won't *need* to try and scare you if you do their job for them."

She sniffed and folded her hands across her chest. The laptop waited for her to finish the half-formed blog post, but she knew she wouldn't be able to focus on it. All of a sudden, the dark, narrow room felt claustrophobic. It was a cage, where she was expected to stay until morning—where the hotel's owners would be free to poke her and torment her like some trapped animal.

Not tonight, creepy hotel owners. Tonight, I write the rules.

Rory plucked her video camera off its tripod and checked the batteries were full. She'd planned to wait until two or three in the morning before venturing out to explore the rest of the hotel, but the suffocative sensation was growing so strong that she thought she might scream if she didn't get some space.

She checked the window a final time before leaving. The

backyard was empty; the ax still protruded from its chopping block. The handle cast a painfully long shadow, but the axman had vanished. Rory crossed to the front door, switched her camera to night vision, and turned the handle.

Cold air skittered over her exposed skin. Rory hesitated on her room's threshold and scanned the front yard for motion. Her car still stood in the driveway, alien and threatening in the dark, but she thought she was alone. Not even the highway's lights were visible.

Rory blew out a slow breath and inched the door closed behind herself. Despite her attempts to keep her footfalls light, she still made more noise than she was comfortable with as she edged along the walkway.

It took only a dozen steps to reach the door to room 7. Rory tried the handle and wasn't surprised to find it was locked. She kept moving to the stairwell and took it to the ground floor.

When she'd gotten her first view of the building, she'd noticed one of the rooms was missing a door. If she had to guess, she would say a previous guest might have broken it—and because months had passed between her and Mistral's last visitor, the room's interior was bound to be a mess. Rory was counting on it. A desolate, environment-damaged room would provide the drama her readers craved.

At the ground floor, she paused to listen. Except for an insect humming in the weeds and a bat's chatter in a far-off tree, the night was uncomfortably quiet. She wasn't naive enough to assume the hotel owners had gone to sleep, but she hoped they wouldn't expect her to leave her room. She didn't want to be caught before she'd documented as much as she could.

The lights in the main building were off. Rory lifted her camera to the windows as she passed and tried to make out the details through the screen. The distorted green view was grainy, but she could see dining tables set with cutlery and glasses, apparently waiting for guests that never came. As she kept moving, she passed a sitting room with a cold fireplace, three lounge chairs, and an empty bookcase.

Rory had started to pan her camera to the outside world when motion froze her. Something had shifted near the back of the room, only its silhouette visible in the poor light. The breath seized in Rory's chest as she squinted at the camera's screen. *Was that the hotel owner? Her husband? Someone else?*

She could no longer see the figure. In the twisted green-tinted world of her camera, all she could make out was the empty sitting room, a curtained window, and a hallway leading deeper into the house.

It might have been the curtains moving in the breeze. Rory licked her lips and tried not to feel how still the air was. *There's no one there. It had to be the curtains.*

A branch snapped, and Rory swiveled to face the forest. The yard was bare, but the pine forest threatened to host infinite invisible figures in its shadowy depths.

Sweat trickled down the back of Rory's neck despite the cold air. Part of her wanted to run back to her room, but a mix of stubbornness and curiosity kept her rooted. *I've visited nearly a hundred supposedly haunted hotels in two years. I'll be damned if this poky little place is the one that beats me.*

Her chest was tight, but she forced air into her lungs. The room with the missing door was close. She refused to run but kept her steps brisk as she strode toward it. The open door was a black, gaping hole, lifeless, soulless, a space that not even the moonlight could penetrate. Rory wanted to hesitate on the threshold, but she knew any pause would allow the creeping misgivings to hook their claws into her. She stepped inside.

Light came through the broken window at the back of the room, but it wasn't enough to bring the space into relief. Rory blindly felt for her camera's buttons and turned on its external light. The beam was smaller and dimmer than she would have wanted, but it worked well enough to expose her surroundings.

The elements had been less kind to the room than she'd expected. Dead leaves were scattered over water-stained carpet. Patchy discoloration—mold or something else, she wasn't sure— grew up the walls. As she approached the bed, she saw the mattress had been pulled off and jammed against the wall near the empty window frame. At first glance, it was possible to imagine it had been used as a barricade. At second glance, Rory felt herself overwhelmed by a deep sense of dread. The mattress had been torn by either a knife or claws, and thick wads of stuffing spilled out like congealed blood from a stabbing victim.

"Can you guys see this?" She spoke in a hushed whisper as she ran the camera's view over the ravaged mattress. "What the hell happened in this room?"

A scraping, dragging noise came from behind her. Rory impulsively pressed the button to turn her camera's light off and swiveled to face the open doorway. She couldn't see anything, and the noise didn't repeat.

It might've been leaves caught up by the wind. Again, she was aware of how calm the night air was. But it was hard to come up with any other explanation. The outside world was so quiet that her ears had adjusted to the near-painful silence. If someone were trying to approach, she would have heard their footsteps.

We'll go in a minute, she promised herself. *We might not even stick around for breakfast—just grab our laptop and jump in the car. Get one or two more minutes of footage and then we're out of this place.*

She flicked the camera's light back on and leaned close so her whispers would be audible. "I thought I heard something outside. I'm not going to lie, guys—this is pretty freaky. I…"

Her voice dropped to silence as she saw a spray of something dark beside the door. She frowned and moved toward it, aware that her hands were shaking so badly that the camera's image would be blurry. There was no mistaking what the stain looked like, though: blood, arcing in a rough line away from the empty doorframe, as though a person had been gutted while trying to flee.

Rory reached a shaking finger toward the marks and brushed one of them. It was dry. Like flicking a light switch, her mind had turned from thinking about taking film for the benefit of her subscribers and moved to the far more awful idea that she might need to hand her recordings over to the police. The rational, grounded part of her mind tried to say it was all an elaborate ruse, that the room had been decorated like a crime scene for her benefit, but the panicked side didn't believe it. *You don't go through all of this effort to impress one small blog,* it said.

Rory slowly lowered the camera to shine its light on the stain on the floor. She'd initially mistaken it for water discoloration, but now, she realized the stain spread into the room. Dribbles led into the bathroom.

Her nerves were begging her to leave, but she took a hesitant step toward the back room. A desperate need to know what the blood led to gripped her and refused to let her go. She needed to see what the shadowed room hid—and record it—even if every second she spent in the building made her prickle like a hundred invisible spiders crept across it.

She moved toward the bathroom. Her camera's weak light provided only brief glimpses of the space at a time: cracked tiles, the sink broken off its pipes and discarded on the ground, the shattered shower door. Once inside the room, she could hear a slow, heavy dripping coming from one of the exposed pipes. Damp air filled Rory's nose and made her snort to clear it.

Her light flashed across the mirror, blinding her momentarily. She pointed the camera toward the ground and squinted. The mirror reflected half of the bathroom, part of the hotel room, the front door…and a tall, unnaturally thin figure standing in the exit.

Rory's heart lurched. She opened her mouth, but fear froze

her. She couldn't even muster the momentum to turn. *Is it the man? Has he been following me?*

He stood perfectly still, blocking Rory's escape, only his silhouette visible in the moonlight. Rory's mind spun out of control. Part of her wanted to confront him, either to demand an explanation for the room's state or to laugh off the situation, but the other half was terrified for her safety. *Someone died in this room,* her mind insisted. *You're going to be next.*

The figure tilted its head. Rory shrieked. At the same moment, the mirror shattered. Spiderweb-shaped cracks spread across the surface, distorting her horrified expression.

She turned, camera held ahead of her body as though it might provide protection. The doorway was empty.

No. Impossible. He was right there—

Her mouth was dry, and nausea tightened her stomach. Only one thought persisted: *Get outside. Get to the car. Get away.*

She took a hesitant step toward the door, blood rushing in her ears, her chest so tight that she thought her heart might be crushed. *Don't go that way,* her subconscious pleaded. *He's waiting for you—ax in hand, probably preparing to mix your blood with the spray already adorning the doorway.*

A soft, cold wind brushed across the back of Rory's neck. She turned to see the window behind her, its glass long fallen from its frame. He wouldn't expect her to leave that way. He wouldn't be fast to give chase.

Rory moved too quickly to second-guess herself. The window was narrow but low; she leaped as she neared it, hit the sill, and rolled over. The hard ground forced the air from her lungs. She bit back a cry and curled into a ball as the rush of pain subsided. The impact would leave bruises, but at least she was no longer trapped in the too-small room.

Get up. Run.

She scrambled to her feet and noticed, with a dull shock, she still held the camera. Its screen had cracked from the impact but it continued to record, and its light acted as a makeshift flashlight.

Rory squinted to see she was in the backyard, not far from the trellises and their ominous shadows. *What's the fastest way to the car? Left?* She turned toward the building's corner and stumbled back. The tall, gaunt figure stood there, one hand resting against the building's stones, barely visible in the darkness save for a flash of light crossing his eyes.

Rory turned and ran. Her breaths came in harsh, quick gasps, and her heart thundered. She saw the chopping block ahead, its ax protruding like a twisted art display, and noticed, with dull surprise, that the handle was covered in cobwebs.

Something snagged around her ankle. Rory cried out as she tumbled to the ground then twisted herself around to face her attacker. She expected to see him looming over her, his wild eyes flashing in the moonlight, but he still stood by the end of the building.

She looked down. Her ankle had become tangled in some kind of wire protruding from the dirt. The loops of metal cord extended through the yard, sprouting up erratically like a deformed, dead weed. Rory tried to kick herself free, but the loops only tightened. She exhaled a curse and dug her fingers under the cord. It was fine but refused to break.

A harsh, repetitive bird screech came from the chicken coop behind her, but the sound was abruptly silenced. Rory lifted her eyes. The man had begun to pace toward her, his long gait lurching and unnatural. She could make out the grizzled stubble and flashing eyes catching in her camera's light, but his expression was unreadable.

"No—" Rory pulled against the cables. They dug into her skin, growing excruciatingly tight.

The man drew ever closer, each step measured and patient. As he passed the chopping block, he reached out to pull the ax free. As it came away from the log, the cobwebs about its handle sloughed off. A thick, dark liquid spread up from the blade's tip, running against gravity until the tool was drenched.

"No!" Rory couldn't breathe, could barely see. She was vaguely aware that a second figure approached from behind. *The wife,* her mind said, but her brain was too clogged by terror to appreciate anything else. She couldn't escape from either figure; all she could manage was to lift her arms to cover and protect her head.

"Be calm," the woman said, and Rory cried out as a heavy hand landed on her shoulder. "I killed a fresh one for you."

Rory peeked from under her arms to see the woman at her side. She thought she might be hallucinating. Blood, bright red even in the thin moonlight, sprayed across the woman's gaunt features. A droplet trickled down across her eye, but she didn't blink it away.

She lifted a twitching, writhing bundle, and Rory saw the woman held a chicken, so recently dead that its legs still kicked. Blood dribbled from the severed neck. The hotel owner raised it above Rory's forehead, and Rory shrieked, trying to twist away from the pulsing, hot liquid running over her.

"We have a contract, my husband and I." The woman's voice was low, but she spoke each word clearly. "He stays on this land and protects me from intruders, but he doesn't touch those who have been marked with chicken blood."

Rory tried to pull away from the chicken, but the hand on her shoulder was a vise. The blood ran down her face, onto her chest, and soaked into her clothes. She spat three words out between clenched teeth. "Let me go."

"Give me your camera." The woman discarded the chicken, its twitching body rolling several feet before coming to rest. The hotel owner held a bloody hand toward Rory, and she placed the camera into her palm.

There was a screeching crack, then the camera's broken shell fell alongside the chicken. "No footage," the woman muttered, then finally released Rory's shoulder. "Now go back to your room. Don't leave again until sunrise."

Rory looked down and saw the wires had vanished—not just from around her leg, but from the yard. The man stood nearby, watching her. Light flashed across his eyes. Then he turned and began walking toward the forest. He'd vanished into the darkness within ten paces.

The strange woman watched her husband leave, seemingly

unconcerned by the blood spattered across her face. Rory held still only long enough to be sure her limbs would obey her, then she was on her feet and scrambling around the building.

She didn't return to her room—not even to collect the laptop—but pulled her keys from her jacket pocket as she raced toward her car. She barreled into the driver's seat, jammed the key into the ignition, and stomped on the accelerator.

As the car screeched down the Mistral's driveway toward the highway, Rory spared the bed-and-breakfast one final glance in her rearview mirror. To her horror, the house had changed. It had once been decrepit; it was now in ruins. Graffiti had been sprayed across the walls, the windows had been broken in, and the roof on one side had collapsed. Decades-old crime-scene tape was crumpled around the area like discarded streamers. And standing at the front door, watching her leave, were the two gaunt, dead-eyed proprietors.

Rory turned her eyes back on the road, her breathing ragged, and focused on speeding back to the safety of civilization as quickly as her car would allow her while the warm chicken blood continued to drip down her face.

AUTHOR'S NOTE

There's something vaguely uncomfortable about independently owned accommodation. Large chain hotels are impersonal. They run by routine, staffed with employees who are waiting for the moment their shift ends and they can switch off from work. When you stay there, you become a statistic; once you leave, you're rarely remembered.

Small hotels are different. They're less polished and more intimate. To the owners, their hotel is not a job; it is a lifestyle. It defines them. It represents a dream, often one that has been worn down and become brittle.

One day, I'd like to write about the impersonal larger chains. They carry their own strain of the unsettling, one that is deeply unfeeling underneath its customer-facing smile. But, for a ghost story, I just had to set it in the smaller, tenser owner-run bed-and-breakfast. Its kind of accommodation has an atmosphere that can't be found anywhere else.

CRAWLSPACE

IT WAS OUR FIRST day in the new house. My parents were downstairs, fighting over how much to unpack. Dad was a borderline hoarder, but at least he was an efficient one. He believed that leaving most of our belongings in boxes would make it easier for next time we moved. We had at least a dozen cartons that were sealed nine years ago, when I was still too young to appreciate the insanity of his logic.

Mom also had hoarder-ish tendencies, but she preferred to have her clutter on display, decorating the house like her personal thrift shop. I was the polar opposite—anything that wasn't absolutely necessary for our comfort or survival could be thrown out. I didn't even have much furniture, just a bed, a wardrobe, a desk, and a chair. My small book collection sat atop my desk, but they were the only decorations I owned. Compared to downstairs—which Mom continued to fill with trinkets, vases, miniatures, and paintings—my room was spartan. I liked it that way.

The lack of furniture meant there was nothing to cover the door in the wall, though. It sat in the area between my bed and my desk. It was barely noticeable unless I was looking for it, but once I'd seen it, the door was hard to ignore.

It's probably empty, I repeatedly told myself as I made the bed and hung my clothes—five shirts and three pairs of pants—in the wardrobe. *It's not like there's some great big secret hidden in there.*

My unpacking took less than ten minutes. I could have gone downstairs when I finished, but I knew I would get roped into helping Dad squirrel away boxes marked "Don't Open," or Mom would ask me to help arrange dozens of her miniature horses and squirrels along the mantelpiece. I'd already done more than my share to help pack them, and the four-hour drive had exhausted me. *If they want clutter in their house, they'll have to deal with the consequences,* I decided and flopped onto the bed.

My window had a view of the large oak tree that grew beside the house, and I watched its fluttering leaves brush against the glass, mesmerized, until I drifted off.

—————

I woke to the sound of tapping. The sunlight was hitting my face, so I rolled over to block it out and mumbled, "I'm coming. Hold on." When the noise didn't stop, I sat up and rubbed my palms into my eyes.

It wasn't Mom knocking at my door, as my half-asleep brain

had assumed. I glanced toward the window, where the motion of the tree leaves had lulled me to sleep. The wind had died down, and the boughs were still.

I mussed my hair out of my face as I looked about the room. The tapping was quiet but, like a dripping tap, impossible to ignore.

"Hello?" I called.

Mom answered me from downstairs. "Dinner's almost ready! Come help me find the cutlery."

As the sound of her voice died away, silence rushed in to fill the space. The tapping had stopped, at least.

It was probably the tree after all.

"Do you want to know what I found out today?" Dad asked.

Our real dinner table was crowded with half-unpacked cartons, so we sat our paper plates on a large packing box while we ate. Neither of my parents seemed to appreciate the irony.

"What?" I asked, scooping up pasta with a plastic spoon.

Dad swelled with excitement. "Apparently, this place used to be an orphanage during the Depression. They had up to sixty children here at a time."

Mom paused, her fork halfway to her mouth. "How did you find that out?"

"Oh, well, I was setting up the office. The computer turned itself on—you know," Dad blustered.

I smothered a grin. I hadn't been the only one slacking off that afternoon.

"The real estate agent said it was built by a lord." Mom put down her fork and smoothed her cotton dress. I was sure she'd been born in the wrong decade. Necessity had forced her to work a part-time job most of her life, but she would have been much happier as a housewife. She even wore dresses and styled her hair as if she were living in the forties. Dad thought she was adorable.

"It was," Dad said, leaning forward. His enthusiasm was contagious, and both Mom and I mimicked his movement to hear him better. "When he died, he left it to a local church, and they converted it into an orphanage. It stayed that way until the eighties, when it was sold and renovated."

"Orphanage, huh?" I asked, glancing about the poky kitchen. "It's not really built for it."

"Well, when you're desperate, you make do with what you've got," Dad said. "There were a lot of homeless children back then, more than any of the orphanages could keep up with, so they crammed the homes to capacity and had the children work— sewing clothes or running errands or whatnot—to help pay for food."

The house was big, much bigger than our last place had been, but it still seemed far too small for sixty children. *Though, I guess, for a parentless child during the Great Depression, you'd call yourself lucky if you had a roof over your head and enough food to keep yourself from starving.*

Mom looked uncomfortable. She'd left her fork in her

half-eaten meal and was rubbing at her arms. "I'm not sure I really like that."

"What's not to like?" Dad asked. He had shoveled so much pasta into his mouth that I could hardly understand him. "We get to be a part of the town's history!"

Mom seemed to be seeing the house in a new light. Her eyes darted over the stone walls and arched doorway, and her eyebrows had lowered into a frown. "I just hate to think about all those children… They must have been so lonely…"

Dad's whole body shook as he laughed. "Lonely? When there were sixty of them? I don't think so."

Mom pretended not to hear him. "That must be why the price was so low. It was even cheaper than that house half its size on Cutty Street, remember?"

"Their loss," Dad said, spearing more pasta onto his fork with a satisfied grin.

***

The tapping woke me in the middle of the night. I lay in bed and watched the opposite wall, where moonlight filtered through the tree outside my window and left dancing, splotchy shapes on the blue wallpaper.

The noise seemed to bore into my skull and knock directly on my brain. I squeezed my eyes shut, willing it to be quiet so I could fall asleep again.

tk tk tk tk tk tk tk tk…

I groaned, rolled over, and pulled my pillow over my ears. It muffled the sound but didn't extinguish it.

tk tk tk tk tk…

If anything, the noise grew louder and more insistent, like a fly that was getting closer and closer to my head. I glared at the shadows cast on the wall, watching as they twitched and swirled, mimicking the infernal tree's movements. Maybe I could convince Dad to cut it down…

tk tk tk tk tk tk tk tk tk tk…

"Shut up!" I yelled, unable to tolerate the tapping anymore. I sat up in bed, feeling flushed, frustrated, and a little ashamed for yelling at a tree.

My room was quiet.

I held my breath, waiting for the noise to resume, but I heard nothing except beautiful, sweet silence. "Huh," I muttered and carefully lay back down. The shadows continued to sway over the wall opposite, but I didn't mind them as long as the noise had stopped. As I closed my eyes and let tiredness claim me, I wondered at how incredible it was that the tree had quietened at the exact moment I'd told it to.

Mom used a hot tray of muffins to bribe me into helping her unpack the next morning, and I spent the first half of the day unwrapping, dusting off, and arranging her miniature collection. She fussed behind me, moving the animals and ball-gown-wearing ceramic women into new arrangements, quirking her head to the side constantly to admire her work.

Finding out she lived in an old orphanage seemed to have shaken her; she was putting even more effort into turning this house into her domain than she had at our last place. She'd rescued her set of doilies and crocheted tablecloths from one of Dad's "Don't Open" boxes and flung them around the sitting room until it looked like a winter wonderland. Even more boggling, she'd brought out some of the Christmas decorations, including our fake wreath, holiday-themed trinkets, and bowls of plastic apples.

"Christmas in May?" I asked skeptically as I poked at one of the glittery apples.

Mom shrugged while she rearranged the miniatures on the fireplace mantel. "I think they look nice. Don't you want our house to be pretty?"

I didn't tell her, but I thought it was bordering on garish. I escaped back to my near-empty room, a pair of hedge clippers clutched in one hand.

Once I'd had a chance to think about it, I'd realized there was a simple way to stop the tapping noise without having to cut down the entire tree. I opened the window, pulled out the screen, and began snipping off all of the branches that touched or came near to the glass.

"I'm going to the shops," Mom called from downstairs. "Does anyone want anything?"

"Thanks, I'm fine," I called back at the same moment Dad hollered, "Beer!"

As I leaned farther out the window to prune branches that were nearly out of my reach, I saw Mom's car reverse out of the driveway and turn toward the town. Just past that, on the other side of the road, an elderly couple was standing on the sidewalk. They watched Mom's car pass them, then both looked back at our house. They'd inclined their heads toward each other and seemed to be talking animatedly.

About us?

Mom would probably get to meet them later when she went up and down the street to introduce herself. The elderly couple didn't look happy, I realized, and I paused my cutting to watch them. The woman had her arms crossed over her chest and was shaking her head, while the man scuffed his boot on the sidewalk. They exchanged another brief word then turned and disappeared into their house.

I found out what my mother's trip to the store had been for when I came down for dinner that night. At least two dozen fat candles had been spaced around the house, shoved wherever there was room between the miniatures. They were scented and lit, and their conflicting odors combined into a horrifically pungent smell.

"What's this?" Dad asked as he followed me through the doorway. His mustache bristled in disgust. "Smells like a perfume salesman died in our damn living room."

Mom sniffed as she dished up plates of fish. Our dinner table was clear of boxes, at least—but now four fat candles were clustered on a doily in its middle. "They're aromatherapeutic," she said. "They'll spread nice vibes through the house."

"This is a horrible fire hazard," I said as I watched a flame lick dangerously close to the wallpaper.

"Well, I'm sorry, but someone has to make this place feel like home," Mom said. She looked offended, so Dad and I dropped the subject.

"I'm going to visit some of our neighbors this evening," Mom said as she placed the plates of steamed fish and greens in front of us. "Does anyone want to come with me?"

Maybe I felt guilty for complaining about the putrid smell of her candles, or maybe it was curiosity about the odd couple I'd seen watching our house, but I found myself saying, "Sure. I'll come for one or two of them."

Mom looked delighted. "Well, I'm glad to see you're taking an interest in your new town, honey. Your father and I are hoping his work will let him stay here for at least a few years this time, so it would be good to make some friends."

"Hmm," I said noncommittally. Dad's work had a bad habit of jumping him across the country at short notice; this was the fifth house we'd stayed at in the last three years. That degree of unpredictability meant making friends was nearly impossible, so I'd just stopped trying. I wasn't holding out much hope that our most recent move would be very different.

I helped Mom wash up while Dad retreated to his office,

ostensibly to catch up on work, even though we could clearly hear him calling out answers to his favorite trivia game show. It was well past dark when Mom finally took up one of the small gift baskets she'd put together and led me out the front door.

"Which house will we start with?" she asked as we paused on the porch, looking at the twilight-shrouded rows of buildings that surrounded our house. "I'll let you pick, honey."

"That one." I pointed to the brick house on the other side of the road, where the elderly couple lived.

The woman answered the door before Mom had even finished knocking. I had the feeling she'd been watching us through one of the white-curtained windows. Her watery blue eyes skipped between my mother and me with a mixture of confusion and curiosity. "Hello?"

"Hello!" Mom gushed, showing her the gift basket. "We're new here. We moved into the house just across the street, and we wanted to say hi."

The woman, who introduced herself as Ellen Holt in between Mom's enthusiastic rambling, invited us inside. The house was smaller than ours, with peeling wallpaper, and it smelled like dust and dead mice. Ellen led us into the living room, where she introduced us to her husband, Albert, and asked if we would stay for a cup of tea.

"I'd love to." Mom placed the gift basket on the cluttered coffee table and settled into one of the lounge chairs. "Honey, why don't you help Mrs. Holt with the tea? Albert, I couldn't help but admire the beautiful vintage car in the driveway. Is that yours?"

166

I had to hand it to her—Mom was a genius at breaking ice. Albert, a thin man with hair just as white as his wife's, seemed to light up at the mention of his Beetle and launched into a lengthy dialogue on it. Mom, who knew next to nothing about cars, smiled and nodded to encourage him.

Ellen led me into the kitchen. I leaned against the counter awkwardly while she filled the kettle, and she shot me a quick smile as her husband's monologue floated through the doorway. "Sorry, Albert loves to talk about his cars."

I chuckled, stared at my folded hands for a moment, then asked, "So, uh, how long have you lived here?"

"Oh, we bought the house when we got married, so…nearly fifty years, I suppose." Ellen pushed her glasses up her nose. "Where did you move from?"

"The city. But we hadn't been living there for long. Work keeps asking Dad to relocate, so…"

"Ah," Ellen said, picking a small jug out of the cupboard. Its inside was coated in dust, but she didn't seem to notice as she poured milk into it. "Do you think you'll be staying here long?"

"No idea." I watched Ellen place four teacups on a floral tray. A cat entered the room, fixed me with its amber eyes for a moment, then rubbed itself against my legs. "I'd like to settle down somewhere, but it's more likely that we'll need to pack up again in six months or so."

"That's not so bad," Ellen said, almost too quietly for me to hear.

"Sorry?"

The older woman paused and seemed to be on the verge of saying something more. Her cat gave a plaintive mewl as it left my legs and began rubbing its head over Ellen's shoes. "I…don't want to alarm you," she said at last, clearly picking her words cautiously, "because there's nothing really to be alarmed about. But…"

"Yes?"

"But you should be careful in that house."

She fished a can of cat food out of one of the cupboards and peeled its metal lid open. The cat redoubled its attentions.

I glanced from Ellen to the living room, where Mom was still pretending to be enthralled in Albert's history of the restorative work he'd done on the Beetle. "Why? Is there something wrong with it?"

"It's…a bit of a strange house." Ellen tipped the cat food into a bowl and bent to place it on the ground. When she straightened again, she fixed me with a searching stare. "I lived here when it was still an orphanage, see? Albert and I used to give sweets and oranges to the children sometimes, when they passed our house. I heard some strange stories about things happening there."

I leaned forward. "Such as?"

"Well, a boy came up to me one morning while I was weeding the garden and said matter-of-factly, 'Henry isn't in the house anymore.' It sounded like he'd just realized it for himself. When I asked what he meant, he said, 'I haven't seen Henry for a month. He didn't get adopted, and he didn't die. I don't think the sisters have noticed yet.' The lunch bell rang, and he ran off before I could ask any more questions."

The electric kettle finished boiling with a click, but neither of us paid it any attention.

"I waited for him to come and visit me again, but he never did. In fact, I didn't see him leave the house at all after that. I don't know if I should have told someone, but I was young back then and didn't want to look nosy. Albert thought the boy had probably found a nice family to take him in."

The cat had finished wolfing down its meal and gave my leg a final rub before leaving for the living room. Ellen kept speaking as she held an empty teapot and stared into the distance. It was as though she'd forgotten I was there, but I was too enthralled to interrupt her.

"Then they converted it back into a home—fresh paint and new doors and all of that—and the owners began renting it out. No one seemed to stay for long, though, a year or two at the most. And it was vacant for long stretches in between too. And then, about eight years ago, I woke up in the middle of the night to find police cars lining the street. A family's child had gone missing. I watched from the window, and all I could think was, *I should have told someone about the missing orphans, then maybe this one wouldn't have gone too.*"

She broke off suddenly, as though she realized she'd said too much, and turned back to me with a shaky smile. "I'm sorry. I didn't mean to yak your ear off. It's not something you should worry about anyway…just an old biddy's imagination getting too excited."

Ellen fumbled to fill the pot, pouring in hot water but

forgetting about the tea bag. I followed her mutely back to the living room and let my thoughts consume me as Mom made enough small talk to cover for both of us.

Henry isn't in the house anymore...

When we got home, I went straight to bed and lay on my back, watching the moonlight's patterns on the wall opposite.

Mom's anxiety about the house having once been an orphanage suddenly seemed much more rational. With sixty children crammed into a house during a time of hardship and suffering, it was beyond wishful thinking to imagine there hadn't been deaths.

I tried to picture what it must have been like while Ellen's story echoed in my head. *I haven't seen Henry for a month...*

If a child—a quiet, unobtrusive, and shy child—suddenly disappeared out of a hectic house with a constantly changing list of occupants, how long would it take before someone noticed?

Was Henry the only child to disappear? What if others had gone missing but were never remembered?

I tossed in my bed, trying to calm my mind enough to sleep. The air felt thick, and I was having trouble breathing properly. Downstairs, Mom's mantelpiece clock chimed one in the morning. I threw off my blankets.

I needed to know more about the house and the people who'd lived in it. My family only had one computer, and it was downstairs, in Dad's office, so I pulled my jacket on over my pajamas and crept out of my room.

The house felt eerily empty and quiet at night. I knew my parents were sleeping in one of the rooms down the hallway, but it was easy to imagine I was the last person on earth as I took the stairs two at a time and turned in to Dad's office.

It was a comfy, cluttered room, and he'd set it up almost identically to the way it had been in our old house. The TV sat in one corner with a couch opposite, and a desk and computer stood against the other wall. The main difference was the stack of boxes pressed into the space beside the couch. Dad was probably still trying to find a place for them.

I turned on the computer and slid into the chair. As soon as the browser loaded, I typed our address into the search bar. The first few results were old real estate listings, but the third link belonged to a historical site. I opened it and started reading.

It must have been the same page Dad had found. It talked about how the house had been constructed in 1891 by a lord who'd owned a good part of the village. When he'd died, he'd gifted it to the local church, which had set up an orphanage under the care of nuns from a nearby convent. When the Great Depression hit, the nuns, who had a policy of helping anyone who came to them, took in far more children than the house had been equipped to hold. There were photos, and I scrolled through them slowly.

Some showed gaggles of scrawny children and teens playing in the yard. Another was of a young girl with thick brown curls, beaming so widely that it looked as if her face might split in half, holding hands with her two new adoptive parents. Another showed how mattresses were stacked in piles during the day, so that the rooms would be usable, then unpacked at night to fill every available space. Even so, it looked as though three or four children had shared each bed, lined up like sardines in a tin.

A blurry photo depicted a nun spooning soup out of a pot that was heated over an open fire outside. *So that's how they coped with the tiny kitchen.*

The final picture showed a different bedroom. The children weren't cramped four to a bed, but each had a mattress of their own. The room looked familiar, but not until I noticed a small shadowy bump in one wall—the secret door—did I realize it was my own room. I scrolled down to read the caption.

Children sick with scarlet fever in the infirmary. As many as one hundred children died at Hallowgate during its time as an orphanage.

"Infirmary?"

I recoiled from the computer as though it had burned me. Looked at the photo again, I saw that the children in the picture were clearly sick. A nun bent over one of the beds, ladling something—water, probably—into a boy's mouth.

I'd seen enough. I powered down the computer, turned off the lights, and slowly climbed the stairs.

It would be easy to move to a different room, I thought as I stood in my doorway and watched the shadows play over the place where dozens of children had struggled, and failed, to stay alive. *It's not like I have to stay here. I only took it because it's closest to the stairs.*

I wondered how angry Mom would be if I disturbed her by deconstructing my room and moving it in the middle of the night. *Probably very.*

C'mon, it's not a big deal. You've slept here before. You can change rooms tomorrow.

I sighed, stepped over the threshold, and closed the door behind myself.

tk tk tk tk tk tk

"Are you kidding me?" I gasped. I was sure I'd cut all of the branches that were close enough to hit my window. I stormed toward the tree's silhouette, pulled open the glass, and looked out.

None of the boughs were even near touching the window. In fact, the air was still, and the tree's leaves weren't moving except for an occasional quiver.

What's the noise, then?

I closed my eyes and focused on pinpointing the infernal tapping. It wasn't coming from outside my room after all, but from behind me. I turned slowly until I was facing the outline of the tiny square door hidden behind the wallpaper.

I felt as if I were in a trance as I walked toward the door. The rhythmic tapping seemed to be growing louder, closer. I knelt on the carpet so that my face was even with the door, and stretched out a hand to touch the surface.

My fingertips tingled where I felt the tapping lightly vibrate the wall. *Like a beating heart,* I thought, as the intensity of the taps increased again. I drew my fingers back then brought my index knuckle forward to rap on the wall three times.

The noise stopped instantly. I held my breath, listening as hard as I could, then I heard three very distinct raps mimicking mine.

I scrambled away from the wall, my heart hammering as I tried to make sense of it.

"Hello?" I called, but my only reply was silence.

A single thought echoed in my head, drowning out logic as it consumed me: *I need to get the door open. Whatever's inside there has to be let out.*

I bolted from my room and raced down the stairs. My footsteps thundered on the wood as I abandoned all attempts to stay quiet. I found a small paring knife in the kitchen drawer and clutched it in my fist as I raced back up to my room.

By the time I knelt in front of my door again, I was panting, and a light sheen of sweat was sticking my pajamas to my skin. I put my head near the wall and called softly several times. There was still no answer, so I pressed the blade into where the wallpaper curved to cross over the edge of the door and began cutting.

The paper was thicker than I'd expected, and it took me several minutes to sever the wallpaper around the entire square. When I was done, I dropped the knife and dug my fingernails into the narrow gap I'd made. I pulled until my fingers ached, but the door stayed fixed in place.

Of course. There's a keyhole. It's probably locked.

I took up the knife again and carefully removed the paper from the bump on the inside of the frame. Behind it was a small bronze keyhole...and I thought I knew where I could find the key that fit it.

On the day my parents had signed the lease for the house, the real estate agent showed us a jar of keys. She'd said no one was really sure which door each key belonged to or which ones were no longer needed because the locks had been changed, but she left it with us in case we ever needed one of them.

As I went down the stairs for the third time that night, I tried to remember where the jar was. I checked in Dad's study first, then in the laundry, and I finally found the old jam jar perched in a cupboard above the fridge. Its collection jingled when I shook it, and I unscrewed it on my way back to my room. I knelt in front of the door, tipped the two-dozen keys onto the floor, and spread them out.

They were all very old. Some were rusted, a couple were bent, and one looked partially melted. It only took a minute to find the key I needed, though. It was smaller than the others, and the bright bronze matched the keyhole. I picked it out of the pile and held it up to the light. It had a delicate, ornate carved design and was small enough that I could have covered it with one finger.

I pushed it into the keyhole. The lock was stiff after years of disuse, but I twisted it as hard as I dared. It unlocked with a gentle click.

The door swung open on its own when I removed the key, finally granting me access to the area beyond. My heart thundering, my palms sweaty, I bent forward to look inside. It was exactly what I'd expected after all: an empty space that went on for several meters before ending in a solid wall.

I rolled back onto my heels and exhaled, uncertain if I felt more relieved or disappointed. If there was no one and nothing behind the door, then the tapping must have been coming from somewhere else—maybe a pipe in the wall that wasn't secured properly or something in the rooms below that echoed into the tiny compartment my door guarded. Either way, I would change my room the next morning and not have to worry about it after that.

I'd half closed the door when something on the room's back wall caught my attention. It looked like white writing on the dark-gray stone. I squinted at it but couldn't make out what it said.

"Jeez," I muttered. I hesitated on the edge of the frame for a beat, then crouched down and started wriggling my torso through the opening. *If I'm going to go to the trouble of opening the damn door, I may as well explore whatever mysteries it offers, no matter how mundane.*

It was a narrow crawlspace. I could reach my hands out to the side a little, but the ceiling was so low that I had to shuffle along on all fours with my stomach only just above the ground. At least it was a short passageway. I reached the end and lowered my chest farther so that I could raise my head and read the writing.

With my body blocking most of the light from the bedroom, I had to shuffle my mass about as much as I could to get illumination.

"Lots…Let's…"

The markings were crude, as though they'd been made by a child blinded by the dark, but once I figured out the main words, I was able to piece together the rest. I read it carefully, making sure I had it right.

176

"Let's…play…hide…and…seek."

The door behind me slammed closed.

I was engulfed in perfect darkness. It was the blackness of nightmares, when you feel like you're drowning hundreds of miles under the ocean's surface, and no matter how hard you kick, you can't see so much as a hint of light. I screamed and jerked, and my head hit the ceiling with a crack. Sharp pain flashed across my skull. I hunched down, pressing my forehead to the ice-cold ground until the worst of the sting subsided.

My ears were ringing—whether from the slamming door or when I'd hit my head, I wasn't sure—and I felt dizzy. I reached a hand toward the wall to the left but couldn't feel it.

That gives me enough room to turn around, at least.

I shuffled in a little circle, trying to get myself facing the door without getting jammed in the narrow confines of the passageway, but not even my feet bumped the walls as I made my turn. I began crawling forward, occasionally touching the ceiling above my head to make sure I was leaving enough room. Then I stretched my hand forward to feel for the door.

One minute…two minutes…

Panic started to build in my chest as I moved farther and farther into the blackness without finding the exit. *It didn't take me this long to get inside, did it?* I kept reaching my hand forward, expecting to feel solid wood but grasping only air. My limbs started trembling from having to carry my body's weight at such an awkward angle. My chest was grazing the floor, and every time I moved forward, my back bumped the ceiling.

It's getting lower, I realized with a stab of shock. *The ceiling is getting lower.*

Panic hit me, and I tried to scream, but even though my throat vibrated, I couldn't hear my own voice. I turned again, trying to find the walls, trying to find anything I could latch on to, but my fingers found no purchase, and every movement seemed to reduce the vertical space I had.

I rotated to face the opposite direction, desperate to find a wall. The stone felt ice-cold under my burning, aching fingertips. The space had reduced so that I couldn't crawl anymore. I had to stretch my hands forward, press my palms to the floor, then use my arms and my toes to drag my body a few inches forward.

I tried to call for help again. Just drawing in the air to yell pressed my chest and my back against the floor and ceiling. Tears began to leak out of my eyes as I gasped. I was suffocating, my arms aching, my head pounding, my skin chilled from where it touched the unnatural stone enclosure.

I had no more wiggle room. My head was tilted, and even by exhaling as deeply as possible, I couldn't get enough space around my body to move. I was trapped in a vise that refused to let go.

tk tk tk tk tk tk tk

I turned my head toward the noise, and my eyes finally found something other than black. A shape was coming toward me out of the darkness—a child.

And yet…the figure was *not* a child.

Its eyes were the clearest; they had no pupil or iris, but they shone at me like huge white disks in the dark. Its face was narrow, gaunt, and unnaturally wrinkled, as though its skin had aged while the flesh and bones underneath remained those of a child. There was no color in its face—I could have been looking at a corpse.

My mouth tried to scream, but my lungs had no room to draw in air.

The child—the *thing*—dragged itself toward me. As its hand extended in my direction, I saw its nails had grown long. When the fingers hit the floor, they made the abhorrent tapping noise that had haunted my stay in the house.

tk tk tk tk tk

I couldn't move. I couldn't protect myself. I couldn't escape. All I could do was watch as the thing that belonged to the darkness scuttled closer.

Henry isn't in the house anymore…

Then I felt them touching me—creatures had approached me from behind, unseen and silent. With their bony, bloodless hands, they grasped my legs and arms, tugging at me, squeezing my flesh, and scratching at my skin. Henry's nails tapped on the ground twice more as he closed the distance between us, and his mouth spread into a toothless smile as he reached out two unnaturally long fingers to caress my face.

I drew in a deep, hungry gasp of air. It was such a shock to be able to breathe that, at first, I didn't realize where I was.

Shadows cast in moonlight by the tree outside my window

danced over the wall, painting beautiful patterns on my wallpaper. I stared at them for a moment then moaned, flipped myself over, and stared at the door.

The keys lay scattered on the ground where I'd left them beside the jar and the knife. The door was open a little, its wallpaper edges jagged from where I'd cut it, exposing a sliver of the nightmare-black inside. The house was quiet, but I thought I could hear my father's faint snores from down the hallway.

I kept my eyes fixed on the doorway. It was almost possible to believe I'd fallen asleep on the floor and dreamed up the hellish tunnel with the slowly lowering ceiling and the decades-old forgotten children…but then, as I watched, unable to look away, the door closed slowly and carefully, until a faint click told me it was locked…and I heard him leave.

tk tk tk tk tk tk tk…

AUTHOR'S NOTE

I wanted to share a short story, *Crawlspace*, which has special significance for this novella. If it weren't for *Crawlspace, Gillespie House* would have never existed.

Short stories come with a unique challenge. Because they have a limited length—7,500 words, according to many publishing houses, before a short story technically becomes a novelette—good ideas often have to be scrapped to keep the story's length manageable.

While I was planning *Crawlspace*, I kept thinking of new scenes and themes, even though I knew I couldn't include them. *Wouldn't it be great to have a graveyard behind the house,* I'd think. *Or a maze of hidden passageways inside the walls. Or a scene where the protagonist explores her home at night. Or, or, or...*

I tried to pare the story down to just the basics, but the excess ideas kept building on each other until there were too many to ignore. I raised a white flag and rewrote *Crawlspace* into what's now *Gillespie House*.

It took nearly two months to plan *Gillespie House*, and during that time, the story evolved dramatically. It changed so much, in fact, that once I'd finished *Gillespie House*, I was able to go back and write *Crawlspace* as a short story, the way it was originally intended to be.

You'll notice similarities between the stories. The initial cause of suspense—the scratching in the walls—is the biggest recurring theme. But I hope you'll enjoy seeing how vastly different the stories became, despite starting from the same place.

LIGHTS OUT

JODIE SWORE UNDER HER breath as she balled her frozen hands into fists and pushed them under her arms, trying to warm them. Her fingers felt like ice that could snap off at any moment. Beside her, Earl lit a cigarette and puffed on it until the smolder took hold. His eyes were bloodshot under swollen lids, and deep crevices around the corners of his mouth told Jodie he was working off a hangover.

On her other side, Miho huddled against the loading dock's brickwork, bundled up in layers of coats and scarves. Her nose was red, barely visible above the fur lining of the jacket she'd pulled up around her ears, and she kept sniffing and rubbing at it with the back of her knitted glove.

Jodie pulled one hand out and checked her watch. It was ten past. She swore again.

"I say we go back inside and let them bring 'em in themselves," Earl said.

"Your dad would have our necks," Jodie retorted. The words came out more harshly than she'd meant them to, but Earl didn't seem to notice.

"I've already told him I'm not working here anymore." He exhaled a cloud of smoke in a slow stream. "I'm a damn laughing-stock, working in a girls' clothing store."

Jodie bit her tongue. The cold was making her want to bicker, but she knew better than to upset the boss's son. Besides, he wasn't going anywhere. He hadn't been able to hold down any other job, and though he said he hated the supposed degradation of being surrounded by fashion, he enjoyed partying too much to give up his only source of income.

"It's here," Miho said with evident relief. She pushed off the wall and started hopping from foot to foot, trying to get some warmth into her legs as she watched the truck backing into the loading dock. Its flashing lights and an intermittent beep warned of its arrival. Earl squinted his eyes closed as though that could block out the sound.

Jodie waited until the truck came to a stop, its rear roller doors facing them, then shuffled toward the cabin. A wave of heat swept over her face as the driver rolled down the window and gave her a toothy grin. "Enjoying the weather?" he asked, passing the clipboard out for her to sign.

"Yeah, it's a gorgeous spring day, huh?" Jodie said, forcing a smile. Outside, the loading dock's doors were obscured by sheets of heavy rain that blurred the outlines of the trees just beyond the parking lot.

"You got it from here?" The driver took the clipboard back. Jodie noticed a well-worn novel on the passenger seat and a refillable mug filled with some steaming substance in the cup holder.

"Yeah, we'll be right." She, Earl, and Miho were already freezing and miserable; there was no point dragging the driver out to help them when he so clearly wanted to enjoy his break in the truck's warm cabin.

Jodie shuffled to the back of the truck again, where Earl had already pulled up the roller doors. Miho stood by with the trolley as Jodie climbed into the back of the truck.

She found eight wooden crates strapped to the truck's floor. As she started to unbuckle them, a chilled sensation that had nothing to do with the cold crawled down Jodie's back. She sometimes got the feeling late at night, when her apartment suddenly seemed wildly too big and too empty for her, and she would pause the TV to listen, convinced she'd heard a door open, and imagine she heard footsteps, foreign and heavy, creeping across the scratched wooden floors.

The sensation was so strong that she stopped, one hand holding the strap's buckle. Her other hand rested on the lid of the crate, which was long, narrow, and large enough for a person to fit inside. *Like a crude coffin.* Jodie dropped the buckle and stepped back, the sensation growing stronger, digging its claws into her chest and gnawing at her stomach. She imagined opening one of the wooden boxes, pushing aside the packing material to find a face, blanched white from death, eyes stitched closed, hands clasped over its suited chest, waiting for her.

"What's'er matter?" Earl slurred around his cigarette. His small eyes were scowling at her as he stood over his own crate. The sound of his voice snapped Jodie back to reality. She took a deep breath and shook her head.

"Nothing. Nothing at all. Let's hurry and get out of this damned cold."

They managed to squeeze four crates onto the trolley, stacking them on top of each other. Earl and Miho stood on either side, bracing the wooden boxes, while Jodie pulled the handle, guiding their cargo through the concrete back passageways of the shopping center.

Their store was in the eastern end of the Inglebrook Center. The complex was nearly two decades old, but scrupulous cleaning and frequent renovations kept it looking brand-new. The public enjoyed polished tile floors, natural lighting via the glass ceiling, and frequent clusters of potted palm trees and shrubs that were so shiny they looked fake upon first glance.

Jodie got to see a very different part of the center, though: the back passageways used by the cleaners and store staff to carry equipment through the building without disturbing the carefully cultivated atmosphere of the public section. There were no polished-tile floors in the back passageways, no potted plants, and no air-conditioning. The back held only concrete, which showed its age with discolored patches and stains, and weak fluorescent lights that cast a sickly glow over the tunnels. Jodie felt like a maid in a historical novel, condemned to use the servants' passageways to travel through her wealthy lord's manor.

"Can you go any faster?" Earl barked. "I'm freezing back here."

"They're ceramic," Jodie retorted, "and I'm not about to explain to the boss that we dropped and broke them."

Earl muttered something under his breath, but Jodie ignored him. They were almost at the door that opened into their shop's cramped storage room. It would be warmer there—and brighter.

"Careful!" Miho shrieked, and Earl shouted a series of expletives. Jodie turned to see that the top crate had shifted, slipping off its pile, and Earl was struggling to get it back on.

"What did I just say?" Jodie snapped, hurrying to help him. For the second time that morning, her words came out harsher than she'd intended, and Earl noticed. He gave the crate a final, hard shove to get it back into place then turned on Jodie, his bloodshot eyes furious.

"It wasn't my fault. Miho pushed it!"

"I didn't!" the girl squeaked from behind the crates. "I was just holding it, and it started falling toward you!"

"Liar!" he yelled back, his voice cracking. "You shoved it really damn hard. You were trying to get me into trouble."

"Enough!" Jodie pressed her numb fingers to the bridge of her nose, where a headache had started. "I don't care what happened. It didn't fall, it didn't break, and Mr. Heinlein has nothing to yell at us about. That's the main thing."

Earl didn't look happy, but he wisely kept his mouth shut. Jodie wrenched their storage room door open and carefully guided the trolley inside. The small area was stuffed with far too much stock; shelves on one wall held bags full of layaway items, and racks were crowded with shirts and dresses that hadn't fit into the front store or were damaged and waiting to be returned. They'd carved a space in one corner by stacking boxes full of clothes and bags up to the ceiling to make room for their delivery. They carefully unstacked the crates, setting them upright in the narrow space.

The door at the opposite end of the room opened, and a small, mousy woman with large teeth poked her head in. "You're back?" She sounded breathless, as if she'd just run a marathon. "Thank goodness. There are at least eight people waiting to be rung up, and the crazy lady's back."

That's the last thing we need today, Jodie thought, smothering a groan.

"I'm going to get the rest of the boxes off the truck." Earl's voice sounded uncharacteristically bright. "Better not keep the driver waiting."

"I'll help you!" Miho took hold of the trolley's handle and pushed it toward the door, which Earl held open, their fight forgotten in their mutual desire to escape the storefront.

Allie, her eyes huge and pleading, hovered in the doorway. Jodie shrugged at her. "Guess it's just you and me. I'll take the crazy lady."

"Thank you," Allie breathed, and darted back into the store. Before following her coworker, Jodie glanced at the crates, which stood just over head height once they were upright. Tall and imposing, the boxes looked even more like coffins than they had on the truck. Their bare, cheap wood took on a strangely gloomy tone in the harsh lights of the storeroom.

Movement caught Jodie's eyes, and she started as one of the crates near the back rocked slightly then stilled. *Probably something in it was settling.*

Jodie hesitated for another moment, her hand on the doorknob, worried that the rocking crate was a sign that they might topple. They held firm, though, stacked like impractically tall dominoes, sending thick shadows running up the walls behind them. Allie called her name, the girl's voice tense with stress under her thin veneer of polite friendliness, and Jodie let herself through the door.

"I'm afraid not," she said for what felt like the hundredth time. She leaned on the store's counter, holding a bag of clothing in front of her. To her right, Allie swiped clothes across the barcode scanner, checking out customers as quickly as she could. Her spiel was the same every time: "Found everything all right? Do you have a rewards account? Cash or card? Would you like a bag for that?"

Mrs. Danvers, their crazy lady, stood in front of Jodie. Her small eyes were watery, their irises so dark that they looked like little pits of coal in her face. She kept licking her lips as though it was a compulsion, while she repeatedly nudged the bag toward Jodie.

"I want to return them," she said, speaking slowly, as though Jodie were too stupid to understand her. "I have the receipt."

Here we go again. Getting Mrs. Danvers out of the shop in under ten minutes was a miracle. They'd been going at it for nearly twelve by that point, and Jodie's patience was wearing thin.

The first time she'd met Mrs. Danvers, she'd assumed the older, overweight woman had a mental disorder. With each visit, though, she'd become more and more convinced that Mrs. Danvers was completely sane but had developed a habit of repeating the same phrases over and over again, like a dog that refused to release its bone, knowing that, eventually, she would win simply by wearing her opponent down.

Not with me. Not today.

"These clothes are outside the month return policy," Jodie repeated, forcing herself to speak calmly, echoing the phrase as though it had become her life motto. "And they show significant signs of wear and tear."

"I haven't worn them," Mrs. Danvers objected, licking her lips again.

"This one has lipstick stains on it." Jodie pulled the clothes out of the bag one by one. "This shirt has a tear down one side. This singlet has stains under the arms. And this skirt isn't even from our store."

Mrs. Danvers turned her head to one side, her shrewd eyes narrowed. "I want to speak with your manager."

"I am the manager." Jodie gripped the bag in both hands to stop herself from giving in to the temptation to shake the older woman.

"I have the receipt." Again, the thick tongue, moist and flabby, slipped out to wet the cracked lips. "I want to return these clothes."

Allie shot Jodie a sympathetic glance as she bagged a customer's purchases. No one liked dealing with Mrs. Danvers. Jodie was the best at it, but she usually had to take a break afterward. She would go into the storage room and punch the bags of clothing or glare at the stain on the ceiling and pretend it was Mrs. Danvers's face while rehearsing the things she would say if there was no risk of being fired. "You're banned from the store for life. Never return!" was always at the top of her list. She was sure Mrs. Danvers had already been blacklisted from most of the other clothing stores in the center. But Mr. Heinlein, their boss, had a strict—and, in Jodie's opinion, idiotic—policy of never turning away customers.

"No," she said, speaking so loudly and firmly that the customers waiting in the checkout line stared at her. "You may not return these clothes. You bought them more than eight months ago, and you've clearly worn them multiple times. You *cannot* return them."

The tongue darted out again. Mrs. Danvers turned her head to the other side, her beady black eyes never leaving Jodie's face. After a moment of thought, she said, "I want to speak to the manager. I need to return these clothes. They don't fit right. I have the receipt."

"No," Jodie said, biting down on the frustration and lowering her voice. "No, no, no, no. You're not returning these clothes."

She waited for the almost inevitable repeat of *I want to return these clothes*, but Mrs. Danvers only stared at her for a moment, looking her up and down, sizing her up to see if she was worth it. Then she reached her fat hands forward and snatched the bag from Jodie. "I'll come back when the manager's in," she said, clutching the bag to her chest, then turned abruptly to the store's exit.

Jodie sagged, feeling exhausted. Allie gave her shoulder a brief squeeze as she hurried past to throw a stack of unbought clothes onto the pile of items waiting to be returned to their hooks.

"Fourteen minutes," she said on the way back, her smile bright and fake. "Could have been worse."

"Hmm." Jodie straightened her back, remembering that the store was full. She wanted to slip out the back and take her ten-minute break to mentally argue with the stain on the ceiling. However, Miho and Earl hadn't returned from picking up the final four crates, and Allie couldn't cope with the rush on her own.

"Can I help you?" she asked the next customer in line, forcing the retail-fake smile onto her face.

Her expression wary, a teenager approached, arms full of skirts that wouldn't flatter her short figure. She'd heard Jodie raise her voice at Mrs. Danvers and clearly didn't want to create a similar scene. Feeling guilty, Jodie widened her smile and put some effort into making it more sincere. "Find everything you were looking for?"

"Thanks so much, guys," Jodie said, pushing through the door to the storeroom. "You were terrific out there, helping Allie and me."

Miho jerked upright, turning red from embarrassment, but Earl remained lounging against one of the few empty patches of wall. He raised his eyebrows. "Crazy lady gone yet?"

"Yes." Jodie sighed and ruffled her hair with her hand. "And the store's quieter now. Allie and Miho are only on shift for another forty minutes, though, so we'd better unpack these suckers quickly before we lose half our manpower."

Miho, looking guilty for hiding in the storage room, hurried to fetch the crowbar Earl had brought into the store that morning. Jodie took the cold steel in her hands and approached the first coffin.

No, not coffin. Crate. Get your head together, girl.

There was no room to lay them on the ground; they would have to be opened while they were upright. It was dangerous, but Miho stood to one side, bracing the crate and ready to catch the contents if they fell out. After pressing the narrow wedge of the crowbar into the gap between the lid and the sides of the crate, Jodie began pulling and pushing, slowly working the nails free. The wood groaned, and one by one, the nails popped free. The gap widened, and Jodie passed the crowbar to Miho so she could use her hands instead. The lid came free after a hard tug, and Jodie pushed it against the wall so she could get at the crate's contents.

The crinkled white tissue paper stuffed inside looked, she thought, like fake flowers purchased at a premium from the funeral home and poured across the coffin's corpse. Then the papers shifted, puffing outward and tumbling toward her as the crate's contents moved. For a second, Jodie thought there might actually be a body inside, buried before it was truly dead, waking up and stretching out of its prison. She smothered a shriek.

As the tissue paper fell away, she caught a glimpse of a mannequin's face, immaculately white, beautifully smooth, and shaped to give the barest impression of human features. The figure, packaged with such care, had overbalanced and fallen forward. She reached out to stop its fall, but it slipped through her hands, landing against her chest instead. The motion swung its arms forward, and they snapped around her, catching her in a lover's embrace. Corpse-cold and chillingly unforgiving, the dummy's hard cheek resting against the nape of her neck.

Jodie staggered backward, shocked by its weight, repulsed by its intimate presence, but terrified of dropping it. She thought the statue tightened its grip on her a fraction, then Miho pulled it off her, babbling apologies while Earl laughed.

"It's fine. It's fine," Jodie said, stepping away from the mannequin. Shaking, she raised her hands to brush over where the statue had pressed against her. *Nothing to be frightened of. You caught it. It's not broken.*

And yet, as she looked at the figure Miho had propped upright, she half wished it *had* broken. There was something unnatural about its face. It was bald, and its features had been shaped to represent a woman; the smooth brow sloped gently until it met the indents where the eyes belonged. The nose was straight and long, a wedge set above stern lips and a smooth jawline. Its head was pointed away, facing the opposite wall, but Jodie felt as though she were being watched. The unusually dark shadows hanging around the indents of its eyes seemed to hide a sidelong glance. She shuddered, even though the storage room was nearly as warm as the main parts of the store.

"Ugly things, aren't they?" Earl sucked on a cigarette with a smug grin, fully aware that the room was supposed to be smoke free. "Dad's such an incredible cheapskate. Apparently, he got them from a store that was closing down in the seedy part of town. He said they were practically giving them away."

"They seem awfully clean if they're secondhand," Miho said. There was something strange about her voice, and Jodie glanced at her. The younger girl had backed away from the mannequin almost as soon as she'd set it upright. Hands crossed over her chest, she chewed on the ends of her hair.

She only does that when she's anxious. Does she feel it too?

Jodie sucked in her breath. She wanted to take a break, go outside, and sit for a while where it was quiet and less claustrophobic, but they had another seven cartons to open before the end of Miho's and Allie's shifts. "Let's get a move on. Earl, take that box out to the bins. Miho, where'd you put the crowbar?"

Jodie opened the rest of the boxes quickly, almost recklessly; her desire to escape the storage room outweighed her anxiety about breaking one of the ceramic statues. The team unceremoniously shoved the mannequins into the corner one by one, and Earl carried each box out after it had been emptied, gradually freeing up room. By the time she was done, Jodie was panting, and her torso was covered in sweat. She threw the crowbar onto an open box of clothes and faced the store's newest acquisitions.

The eight mannequins—two male, six female—faced her with identical inscrutable expressions. Their long white arms were outstretched, their stiff fingers angled into strange gestures. The light shone off their perfectly smooth skin, and Jodie thought back to what Miho had said about them being unusually clean for secondhand. They were more than clean; they were flawless. Jodie would have expected them to have sustained at least *some* damage at their old store, but she couldn't see a single scratch, chip, or crack. She didn't like the way it made her feel.

She checked her watch; Allie and Miho would be off shift in five minutes. "Better get them into the store and throw some clothes on them before you go."

Jodie approached the nearest one, a woman, and hooked her arms around the mannequin's chest. It was much heavier than she would have expected, and she strained to lift it and carry it toward the door. She eased her way into the front of the store then dragged the mannequin to a corner of the room to stand it next to one of their old dummies.

The replacement mannequins were long overdue. The old figures, which had been thirdhand when Mr. Heinlein bought them, dated back to the '60s and showed their age. They were scratched, chipped, and grimy around their joints. Two of them had limbs stuck on with duct tape. Jodie had, after months of gentle nagging, convinced the boss to invest in new ones.

She glanced between the two figures. One was horribly dirty, missing two fingers and nearly a third of the white paint on its face. Its torso was a little too large to hold the clothes well. The other looked brand-new, immaculate, and perfectly formed. Still, Jodie suddenly wished they could keep the old ones.

She stripped the clothes off the old mannequin and pulled them onto the new figure. She hated the feel of its ceramic skin and moved as quickly as she could. When she was done, she dragged the old dummy into the storage room, where Miho and Earl had already finished two.

Jodie picked up another of the new mannequins and pulled it back into the storefront, aiming for the display windows. A middle-aged woman with short hair—one of their regulars—was riffling through a rack of discounted clothes. She smiled at Jodie as she passed. "Finally got some new models, eh?"

"Yeah," Jodie panted, trying to smile despite the crawling feeling covering her arms and back. "About time, huh?"

"They'll certainly brighten the store a bit." The woman moved away from the rack of clothes to watch Jodie set up the manne-quin, and the expression on her face changed as she got a good look at the statue. Jodie was halfway through pulling the old mannequin's sweater off when she glanced at the woman. Her face had changed from bright warmth to confusion, and as Jodie watched, it morphed into concern.

"Everything okay?" Jodie asked, pulling the sweater free. The woman had turned her head to the side to watch the mannequin out of the corners of her eyes and, at Jodie's voice, started.

"Oh, yes, thanks. I just…I'm supposed to meet my husband in the food court. I'd better go. Don't want to be late."

"Sure." Jodie, nonplussed, watched the woman leave the store with long, fast strides, disappearing among the milling shoppers in seconds. She turned to look at the mannequin, again feeling the unnerving sensation of being watched. She frowned and threw the sweater over the flawless white head.

***

"Seriously?"

Earl jolted and moved to hide the bottle, but Jodie stalked around the desk to where he was crouched and snatched it from him.

"Tubbi Wine, huh? What? Doesn't this job pay enough for a decent brand?"

"Give that back," Earl snarled, getting to his feet, his face twisted in frustration. "It's nearly the end of shift anyway—"

"So you thought you'd get a head start on tonight's plaster session?" Furious, Jodie shoved the bottle back into his hand. "Nuh-uh. Not on my watch. I'm not working with a drunk."

She was aware her voice had that hypercritical edge again, but she couldn't stop. The afternoon shift, despite being unusually quiet, had exhausted her more than the weekends did. It was the mannequins; she kept turning, sure that someone was in the store, watching her, only to find herself facing one of the statues. *You're just not used to them,* she kept telling herself. *In a week, they'll be so familiar that they won't bother you anymore.*

"Have you even swept the floor?"

"Sure I did." Earl had adopted the sulking, saggy expression she'd come to loathe. He raised the bottle to his lips and took a drink, glaring at her with his small, dark eyes.

Jodie breathed deeply through her nose, trying to quash the anger that threatened to spill out. "You could've fooled me. The floor's filthy."

Earl shrugged and screwed the bottle's cap back on.

It was just past their five thirty closing time. Jodie glanced about the store, taking a quick assessment of what still needed to be done. The floor needed sweeping; that was Earl's job. The trash can behind the desk was overflowing with unwanted customer receipts and price tags, also Earl's job. Stock needed to come out of the back room to fill up the empty slots on the racks, two layaways needed filing in the back room, and the security system had to be set on the way out. *Earl, Earl, Earl.* The only completed tasks were hers.

Jodie, aware that she was seconds away from slapping her coworker, pulled her gloves on with harsh tugs. "Okay, I'm going home. You can close up on your own tonight. Ass."

Earl called her a very unflattering name in response, but Jodie pretended not to hear him as she stalked to the shutter on the front entrance and raised it just enough to slip underneath. A dozen stragglers were still meandering through the center, either on their way to their cars or waiting for a movie. She could hear a shutter closing a little way off as another employee locked the doors to a nearby store. Turning left, toward the nearest exit,

Jodie walked as quickly as she could, glad to be out of the store for the day. And not just because of Earl.

Miho was waiting for Jodie outside the shop the following day, yawning and huddled in her jacket. Jodie's morning had been filled with disaster, from lost car keys to catching every red light between her house and the shops, and her shift should have started ten minutes before. "Sorry I'm late," she said, hurrying to find the store's key in her overfull key ring.

"'s fine," Miho mumbled, shifting from foot to foot, either to keep warm or stay awake. "I forgot my keys at home."

Jodie pushed the key into the shutter's lock and frowned. The lock didn't turn like it normally did. She pulled on the shutter and swore as it rose without resistance.

"What's wrong?"

"Earl didn't lock the doors last night." Jodie pushed them up, locked them into the slot in the roof, then swore again when she saw the inside of the store.

Earl's now-empty bottle still sat on the counter. The broom was propped against the jewelry stand, though the floor hadn't been swept, and bundles of clothes had been draped across the store's racks. Worse, the mannequins had been stripped of their clothes, which lay in clumps on the floor.

"Unbelievable," Jodie hissed, stalking into the store. "He's going to get an earful this afternoon."

She started snatching the clothes off the dirty floor and pulling them back onto the mannequins. Miho picked up the empty bottle and frowned at the label, chewing the ends of her hair again. "Do you think he has a problem?"

"Oh, he's got a problem, all right. And its name is Jodie."

Miho laughed, and Jodie felt herself relax. She liked working with Miho; the girl was quiet and unpresumptuous, and she worked hard. *Unlike some people I know.*

"Quick, throw that bottle away so the customers don't see."

Jodie began re-dressing the mannequins Earl had stripped while Miho tossed the bottle into the storage room and gave the dirtiest parts of the floor a quick sweep. The shopping center was filling up as the stores opened, and their first customer came in just as Jodie shoved a cap onto one of the male mannequin's heads in a failed effort to make it look less sinister. The woman flicked through a rack near the door for a few seconds before drifting out without buying anything. Three more customers quickly replaced her then left again in under a minute. As Jodie hurried through her morning tasks, she noticed more and more customers were entering the store then leaving almost immediately. Casual browsers weren't uncommon, but at least a few would always stay for a while and try on some of the clothes.

It was so unusual that Jodie found herself counting how many seconds each of the shoppers lingered. A regular customer stopped at one of the discount racks. The woman flipped through the shirts then started as though something had alarmed her. She swung to face the mannequin behind her and stared at it for a moment before hurriedly pushing the shirt she'd been holding back onto the rack. Her aim was off, and the hanger and shirt clattered to the floor, but she didn't stop to pick it up as she pulled her jacket about herself and strode out the door.

"Did you see that?" Jodie asked, but Miho, who had been arranging the shoes on the shelf beside the desk, only looked at her questioningly.

Feeling uneasy, Jodie approached the discount rack. She faced the mannequin and searched its blank, soulless face, trying to find what had disturbed the customer. The statue only gazed back, expressionless, inscrutable. Jodie turned and picked the dropped shirt off the floor. *Of course, it's in the one place Miho didn't sweep.* She grimaced, trying to brush the dust and bits of fluff off the fabric, then froze.

The strangest sensation came over her, the same one she'd felt in the truck, when she'd hesitated over the coffins—*the crates.* It also came over her very late at night or in the early hours of the morning, when she was walking home and couldn't shake the feeling that she was being followed through the empty streets; she would put her hands in her pockets and quicken her step. Jodie was never brave enough to glance into the dark alleys that ran between the buildings like empty veins, though she would swear she heard a second step masked by the echo of her own hurrying feet.

She turned slowly, not wanting to see what was behind her but too frightened to do otherwise. The mannequin stood where she'd left it, its face wearing the same empty expression, its hands still raised in odd gestures. It seemed different somehow. More aware. *Awake.*

Stop it. Stop it, stop it, stop it.

"Jodie?" Miho called from behind the desk. "Something wrong?"

The customers felt it, too, Jodie realized, staring at the mannequin and feeling, with overwhelming certainty, that it was staring back.

Then laughter, raucous and mocking, shocked her, and she was finally able to break the gaze. A gaggle of teenagers had gathered in the male-wear corner of the store, where they were yelling and pushing each other.

"No, really, dude," a pale, scrawny one said, his loud voice easily carrying across the store. He was shifting in agitation, hopping from foot to foot and shaking his arms to make his duster flap. "It *blinked*."

"*Dude*," his companion said, stretching out the syllable and leaning on the nearest rack for support as he struggled to stop laughing. "It doesn't even have *eyes*. Just how high are you?"

Jodie approached them without being aware that her feet were moving. Her mouth was dry and had an odd taste, and tension spread across her shoulders. "Can I help you?"

The teenagers looked at her and laughed. "Naw," the tallest one said, slapping his pale companion on the back. "We're going."

Jodie felt frozen to the ground as she watched the teens leave with the peculiar loping gait that their social circle always seemed to favor. The pale one started laughing along with his companions as they mocked him. Slowly, Jodie turned to look at the mannequin they'd been standing beside. It was the one she'd thrown a cap on. The cap had only succeeded in darkening the shadows under its eyes, once again giving her the sensation that it was watching her through the shrouded depths.

"I'm taking a break," Jodie said, crossing the store so quickly that she knocked several clothing racks askew. "Be back soon."

Without giving Miho a chance to answer, she jogged into the storeroom and closed the door behind herself. Her hands were shaking, and the tightness over her shoulders had spread down her chest and knotted in her stomach like a cold, thick snake coiled in her abdomen.

The storage room felt comforting, though. Its haphazard stacks of boxes overflowing with clothes, the shelves crammed full of lay-aways, and even the garbage bag left by the door were mundane, safe, and familiar. Jodie sank to the floor and pulled her knees up under her chin, closing her eyes and breathing deeply. Her heart rate slowed, and strength gradually eased back into her limbs.

What's gotten into me? She listened to the muted noises coming from behind the door that led to the main part of the store. *They're only mannequins. Yeah, they're creepy, but they're not actually* doing *anything. Except for maybe bankrupting the store.*

Calm washed over her as the tension left her shoulders and the sweat dried. She thought of Earl, who would be coming in for his shift that afternoon. She hoped he wouldn't give Allie any trouble. If he tried to drink during work again, she would have to tell the boss—and she wasn't looking forward to it. Earl's father was surly, and although he wasn't fond of his son in any sense of the word, he hated criticism.

Maybe I could move on. I might need to anyway, if the mannequins are scaring the customers away. I could start putting out résumés again. Maybe actually make it into the journalism field and get some use out of my degree. Wouldn't that be amazing? I could get out of this awful store and away from Earl and Earl's father and the new mannequins—

The door creaked open, and Miho's round face peered through. "Jodie? You okay?"

"Yeah, fine." Jodie found her words were almost true. "Need help out front?"

"The crazy lady came in," Miho said.

Jodie sighed and got to her feet. "Sure, I'll take her—"

"But she left again."

"What?" Jodie went to the door and looked out. The store was completely empty.

Miho shrugged, chewing on her hair. "She stood by the discount rack for a minute then left. Didn't even *try* to talk to me."

"Huh." Jodie looked toward the rack and the tall mannequin wearing slacks and a hoodie that stood beside it. She could guess why Mrs. Danvers hadn't lingered. *Maybe those mannequins have some perks after all.*

Jodie sat behind the desk, tapping a pen on the scratched wooden surface as she surveyed the empty store. Calling it a slow day would have been an understatement. She'd kept herself busy dusting shelves and rearranging clothing racks, but without any customers, there was nothing else to do. Miho had gone home, and Allie, whose shift had started ten minutes previously, was drifting among the racks, looking lost.

"And it's been like this all day?" she asked on her third lap around the store.

"Pretty much. One woman came in to exchange her shirt for a different size. Otherwise, nothing."

"Maybe it's the weather."

The rain from the previous day had continued through the morning as a drizzle, but Jodie doubted that was to blame for their deserted store. "Maybe."

She checked her watch. It was ten minutes past the end of her shift, but Jodie was waiting for Earl. She'd spent the morning rehearsing what she wanted to say to him—in a calm, moderate voice, she'd promised herself—but he was, predictably, late.

He must know I'm angry about the state he left the store in last night. He's probably hoping he can wait long enough for me to leave and avoid the lecture.

"This is ridiculous," Jodie grumbled. She picked up the desk phone and dialed the cell number written on a Post-it Note hidden just out of the customers' sight. It rang four times before going to voicemail. She hung up without leaving a message. "He's not answering."

"Maybe he's driving here right now," Allie said, shaking out the top shirt on its stack and refolding it.

"Maybe," Jodie said. Earl couldn't afford a car, and his father refused to lend him the family vehicle, so he took public transport on days he couldn't get a lift.

A customer drifted in through the doors then floated out like a leaf caught in a swirl of wind. Her large teeth worrying at her lower lip, Allie watched the woman go. "Well, you might as well head home. Even if Earl doesn't come in, it's not like I'm going to be overwhelmed."

Jodie pursed her lips. She hated the idea of letting Earl win, but his stalling tactics were gradually eating away at her afternoon off. She'd already made plans that involved the three latest episodes of her favorite show, an extra-large blanket, and Chinese takeout. "Thanks, Al, I might do that. Look, Earl was acting up last night. I caught him drinking behind the desk, and he left the store unlocked. If he gives you any sort of trouble today, give me a call, all right?"

"Will do."

Just before nine in the morning, the clouds from the previous two days had parted to offer a little weak spring sun. The weather forecast had said another storm was coming that evening, though, but Jodie had been thinking there might be just enough time to dry the laundry before her shift that afternoon. She was nearly done when a bright jingle disturbed the silence and sent Jodie searching her pockets for the phone.

She glanced at the number and recognized the work landline. *Who's scheduled this morning? It's Miho and Earl, isn't it? Or maybe someone else is calling…*

The sensation of something being not quite right was so strong and so sudden that it knocked the breath out of her lungs. The morning didn't seem bright anymore, but cold and alien. In her mind's eye, she saw a hand reach for the clothing store's phone on the worn wooden bench, pick up the receiver, and dial her number. But the hand wasn't flesh and blood. The perfectly white porcelain fingers that should have been frozen moved dexterously as they danced over the number pad—

Then the phone rang again, and Jodie shook herself out of the stupor. The work number still flashed on the screen, and she pressed the answer button. "Hello?"

"Jodie, thank goodness!" The notes of fear and anxiety in Miho's voice doused Jodie's momentary relief.

"What's wrong?" She dropped a wet shirt into the washing basket.

Miho hiccuped then took a steadying breath. "I think we've been robbed."

"What?" Jodie was already jogging into her house to find her car keys. "Are you sure?"

"Pretty sure." Jodie pictured Miho standing behind the counter, holding the phone's old-fashioned receiver in both hands as she surveyed the store. "The doors weren't locked again. And there's stuff everywhere—pulled off shelves, off racks. It's a disaster."

"Hang tight. I'm on my way." Jodie hung up as she slid into the driver's seat of her car and turned the key in the ignition. Her mind was racing, trying to make sense of it.

The doors were unlocked... Only five people had keys to the store: Jodie, Allie, Miho, Earl, and Mr. Heinlein. Allie and Earl had been on closing shift the night before. Her first thought was that Earl had gotten drunk again and left the doors open, but she'd warned Allie about it the previous afternoon. Allie was too much of a worrier to let Earl close up shop alone anyway.

"Jeez," she hissed, weaving through traffic a little too quickly to be safe. She tried to think about how much might have been lost; it was a low-price store, and their most expensive pieces cost sixty dollars, so a thief couldn't have made off with a fortune. Mr. Heinlein would be furious, though, no matter how small the loss was.

Jodie parked haphazardly and jogged through the near-empty center. Miho was waiting just inside the store, and one look at the girl's face told Jodie the last ten minutes had been hell.

"Hey, it's okay." She put an arm around Miho's shoulders and gave them a squeeze. "You're not hurt, are you?"

Miho shook her head, but her face was still scrunched up. "The store—look at it—Mr. Heinlein—"

"It's not your fault. He won't get angry with you." Jodie gave the girl's shoulders another squeeze then stepped forward to survey the damage.

Miho hadn't been exaggerating—it was a disaster. Virtually every shelf was empty. The shirts, the jeans, the dresses, the jewelry, the skirts, and the shoes all lay in piles on the floor. A few items hung from the top of the shelves, and one scarf dangled from a ceiling light. Most of the clothing racks had been overturned, and the T-shirt table had been jammed into the corner. Most of the mannequins had been knocked over. It hadn't been casual riffling; it had been pillaging.

"I didn't touch anything," Miho said, watching Jodie, who was turning in a slow circle to examine the room. Despite the gravity of the situation—or perhaps *because* of it—Jodie had to bite down on a laugh. She could imagine Miho saying exactly the same thing to a pair of police officers at the scene of a violent murder.

"Okay." Jodie pressed her fingers to the bridge of her nose as she thought through their options. "Close the doors, Miho. We can't let customers into the store like this. I'll call Allie."

She gingerly stepped over the sea of discarded clothes to get to the checkout table while Miho pulled down and locked the shutter. Customers would still be able to see through the windows—and, in fact, a couple of curious faces were already peering through the empty display at the other end of the store—but at least they wouldn't be interrupted while they assessed the damage.

Jodie dialed Allie's number from the Post-it Note then shifted from foot to foot as she waited. The phone rang four times before going to voicemail. Jodie hung up and tried again, with the same result. She sighed and waited for the beep. "Allie, call work, please. It's urgent."

Next, she tried Earl's number. Again, her call went to voicemail.

She didn't bother leaving a message. It was quarter past nine, which meant he was probably skipping work...*again*.

Finally, she called Mr. Heinlein's number and scowled when his phone, too, rang out. No answering machine took the call.

Miho was hovering beside the desk, chewing at the ends of her hair. Jodie gave her a helpless shrug. "Well, we did inventory last week, at least. That'll help us figure out what we're missing. Better get started."

The cleanup consumed the entire morning. Jodie stood at the desk, comparing sales receipts with their inventory to come to an approximate tally of what they were supposed to have, while Miho picked the clothes off the floor, checked them for damage, and rehung them. Once Jodie's list was complete, she joined Miho. Her back ached by the time they stopped for lunch.

"We're getting there, at least," Miho said from her perch on the corner of the desk, eating the kebab Jodie had treated her to. They'd rehung almost all of the scattered clothes but hadn't counted them yet.

Jodie checked her watch. "It's nearly the end of your shift. D'you want to go home? I doubt we'll be able to open today, anyway."

Miho shook her head quickly, and strands of her sleek black hair stuck to the grease around her mouth. She rubbed them away with a grimace. "Nah, I'll stay and help out here, at least until Allie comes in."

Jodie was anxious for Allie's shift to start too. The five calls she'd placed throughout the morning had all ended up in voicemail, and they still hadn't been returned.

If she could just speak to Allie, she would at least know who was responsible for the damage. Allie or Earl might have dropped their key somewhere, giving a thief easy access to the store, or Earl had possibly gotten plastered and invited some of his buddies in to help him pull apart the shop he hated.

Jodie tossed her own kebab wrapper into the bin and hopped off the corner of the bench. The mannequins still needed righting; she's been putting it off, but with the rest of the store mostly sorted, she couldn't ignore them for long. They'd been stripped, just like the night before, and Jodie picked up the first one gingerly.

The white face stared down at her as she righted it. Even after being thrown to the ground, the porcelain was blemish free. Jodie found herself staring at it, searching the skin for imperfections—a hairline crack, a smudge, anything to abolish the niggling idea that the statues couldn't be damaged—but as her eyes darted over the face, she felt as though she were being scrutinized in return. In that moment, she became convinced that the lips weren't set in a neutral expression but that they were *smirking*. The face wasn't blank; it was arrogant and intense.

She swiveled the mannequin away so it faced the opposite direction and dressed it as quickly as she could manage with shaking fingers.

Jodie knelt on the cold tiles, shaking out the tangled necklaces and bracelets that had been knocked off the jewelry stand. Every thirty seconds, she paused to check her watch then glanced at the shutter door before frowning and returning to the jewelry. Two minutes past the start of Allie's shift, she still hadn't arrived.

Allie was notoriously punctual. Everyone else—including Jodie—occasionally missed the start of a shift, except for Allie. She sometimes arrived as much as half an hour early if she'd heard traffic was likely to be bad.

A tight ball of anxiety began to build inside Jodie's chest. What-if scenarios fluttered through her head, and they became increasingly difficult to push aside. *What if*, instead of being busy, she'd been unable to answer her phone? *What if* the break-in had happened while Allie was still in the store? *What if* she was in trouble, hurt, or worse? Jodie's fingers faltered as she tried to pry apart a necklace and a watch, then she threw them onto the floor in frustration.

Since Mr. Heinlein hadn't answered her first call that morning, she'd been reluctant to call again, partly because he tended to shoot the messenger and partly because she'd been hoping to finish the inventory and have exact details for him before delivering the bad news. But Mr. Heinlein held the contact details for Allie's family, and he was Jodie's only other link to Earl, who might be able to shed light on what had happened the night before.

One hand on the receiver, she hovered behind the desk, breathing deeply and wishing Allie would just *turn up* so she could delay the call for another few hours. The eyes were on her again; it seemed like every mannequin in the store had a direct line of sight to her. Their attention was fixed on her movements: the way the lump in her throat made her grimace when she swallowed and how her eyes couldn't stay still. They were anonymous spectators, faintly amused, and she was their entertainment for the afternoon, a dull little distraction for them to judge at their leisure.

Jodie squeezed her eyes closed, trying to block out the faces and struggling to clear her head. She took a sharp breath then bent over the bench to obscure the mannequins' view. Jodie dialed Mr. Heinlein's number.

He answered after two rings with his characteristic "What?" Based on the way he slurred the word, Jodie thought he must have had a cigarette in his mouth. *Either that or he's drunk.* She braced herself and described the situation as briefly and factually as she could.

She tuned out a lot of what he said after that. He uttered copious swear words, most of them directed at her, and vague threats of suing for negligence. He also asked a series of questions she had no way of answering: "How much is this going to cost me? Huh?" and "Who's responsible? Who the hell did it?"

Jodie stared at her watch through the ordeal, letting her attention focus on the beautifully predictable second hand twitching its way around the dial. It was eight and a half minutes past by the time Mr. Heinlein's anger had ebbed enough for her to move the conversation along.

"Allie's shift was meant to start ten minutes ago, but she's not here. Has Earl said anything about—"

"Haven't talked to Earl," Mr. Heinlein spat, sounding disgusted. "Not for a couple days. We had...*an altercation*, so he's gone to sulk at one of his idiot friends' house."

That would explain why he hadn't been to work. It might also have been his motive for destroying the store, if he really was responsible.

"Well, I can't contact Allie. I'm worried something's happened to her."

"Maybe she's run off with my son," Mr. Heinlein said, and Jodie cringed as his cold laughter broke into a hacking cough.

"The police should be contacted." Jodie grimaced, knowing Mr. Heinlein had a deep-seated hatred for their local police.

"What the hell for? You want to cause trouble for the store? Is that what you're doing?"

She could feel the mannequins' amusement. They were gloating, mocking her for turning to such an unstable ally. Jodie turned her back to them, facing the wall behind the counter, where a giant poster of a woman wearing fashions nearly five years old was stuck. Every time Mr. Heinlein tried to divert the argument, Jodie repeated, "Allie's missing. Someone should be contacted." It became a mantra, which she interjected anytime her boss paused to take breath.

I've turned into Mrs. Danvers. Hysterical laughter rose inside her, forcing her to bite her cheek to keep it contained.

"Fine," he snarled after she'd said the phrase for the fifth time. "I'll call her family, and if they haven't seen her, I'll tell the police, and they'll probably shut the entire store down for a month while they figure out she skipped town with a drug-addict boyfriend. Happy? Now get my store fixed."

He slammed his receiver down, and the crack echoed in Jodie's ears long after she'd replaced her own receiver on the cradle. She turned back to face the store, and the mannequins, and forced a ghastly smile onto her face for Miho's benefit as she returned to the jewelry rack.

At nearly four in the afternoon, they finally finished the inventory. Jodie ran through the numbers one last time, incredulous. The stock left in the store perfectly matched the list of what they were supposed to have. If there'd been a break-in, the thief must have spent upward of an hour tearing the place apart then left without taking so much as a bangle.

"That's good, isn't it?" Miho leaned on the desk, looking drained. There were dark circles under her eyes, and the ends of her hair were split from her chewing on them.

Jodie gave her a sympathetic smile. "I guess it is. Head on home. I'll call Mr. Heinlein then close the shop early. We can re-open properly in the morning." She hesitated. "I know tomorrow was meant to be your day off, but…"

"Yeah, of course I'll come in." Miho sounded bright, despite her exhaustion. "None of my classes this week are really important, anyway."

"Thanks." Keeping the store open with both Allie and Earl

gone would mean a lot of extra work, and Jodie hated the idea of having to spend time alone with the mannequins. Even just having half a day of company would be a huge relief.

Jodie ushered Miho out under the shutter door then pulled it back into place. She glanced around the store, feeling the solitude acutely, and tugged her jacket around her body as she made for the phone beside the desk.

Mr. Heinlein answered almost immediately. Not only had he calmed down since the first call, but the news that his stock was intact actually made him cheerful. "Good thing too," he grunted. "Can't afford to buy in anything else until the start of the new season. They cost us a day of business, but we'll recover from that."

Jodie licked her lips. The mannequins were watching her again, their empty eyes fixed on her as she paced behind the desk. "Did you get in touch with Allie's family?"

"Yeah, a dead end. Her contact was her father, who died last year."

"And then you called the police, right?"

Mr. Heinlein's guilty silence stretched out, and Jodie snapped, "She's not answering her phone, and she missed her shift. She could be in serious trouble—"

"Fine," he snarled, then ended the call before Jodie could say another word.

Jodie threw the receiver onto the desk, disgusted and furious, and looked up at her audience of mannequins. "What?" she snapped at the rows of faces then turned and half walked, half ran to the supply room and pulled the door closed so sharply that the thin wall shook.

Frustration and fear for Allie collected inside of her, knotting into a painfully hot ball inside her chest. She pressed herself into an empty space between the shelves and an open box of defective sequined shirts and pressed her hands over her face.

She hadn't needed to work a full day in the store for a long time, and the constant bending and stretching had set a dull ache in her lower back. The storage room was comforting and safe. She was warm, and the sequined shirts under her cheek were unexpectedly comfortable. The store waited for her beyond the storeroom door, filled with the impersonal mannequins, and instead of mustering her strength and returning to them, she let her eyes close. *Just a moment's rest. Then we can go home.*

Jodie started awake, heart racing, palms clammy. After a second, she realized she was still huddled in the corner of the storage room. Grimacing, she rubbed at the side of her face where the sequins had bitten into her skin. The store was completely silent. Something had disturbed her, though, and she struggled to remember what it was. Some sort of beep…

She found the source after a moment. A cell phone had been left on one of the shelves, propped against a box of bags bearing the store's logo, and the message icon was flashing. Its owner might have set it down for a moment while putting a coat on or retying a shoe and forgotten it.

Jodie guessed whose phone it was and swiped it on to make

sure. Sure enough, the background was a photo of Allie's cats. There were eight messages. Five would have been from her; the rest must have come from friends or relatives.

That explained why the calls hadn't been returned, at least. And if Allie used her phone's calendar to keep track of when she was working, she might have easily forgotten that she'd been scheduled for the afternoon shift. The anxiety in Jodie's chest eased slightly, and she replaced the phone and rubbed at her sore eyes.

It was just after seven thirty, which meant the only shops left open would be the grocery store at the end of the center and the movie theater in the food court. Jodie pushed through the storeroom door and back into the main part of the shop.

It was pitch-dark. The only light came through the windows, from the shopping center's large ceiling lights, and they were at the wrong angle to reach far into the store. Jodie hesitated. *I left the store lights on, didn't I?*

After her call to Mr. Heinlein, she'd been too angry to do anything except storm into the storage room. Perhaps one of the security guards had passed by, thought the store was empty, and turned the lights off for her. *Impossible. They wouldn't have a key to get inside.*

Except…she hadn't locked the door after letting Miho out. Jodie hurried through the store, weaving past the racks and tables that were only barely visible, to reach the shutter. She gave them a tug, but they held fast.

Whoever had turned off the lights must have had a key, then, to lock the door. *Did Miho come back? Allie, possibly, or even Earl?*

Jodie turned to squint at the room. The ten mannequins, barely visible shadowy figures, were spaced around like sentinels, some half-hidden behind their racks, others posed on their stands by the windows.

Wait…ten?

Jodie recounted them quickly, and her heart rate shot up. There were definitely ten figures in the store. And yet, they'd only received eight crates.

Her mouth was suddenly dry. She moved quickly and quietly, not daring to take her eyes off the room, which suddenly felt claustrophobic, as she sidestepped toward the light switch by the door. Her foot landed on something soft, and she hopped back, horrified. It was a T-shirt, casually discarded.

Did we miss one of the shirts when we cleaned the place? No, we couldn't have. We were too thorough.

Jodie reached out a hand and fumbled for the switch beside the doors. It turned on with a quiet click, and light filled the room. Any thought of two of the shadowy figures being intruders disappeared with the darkness. They were all mannequins, their flawlessly smooth faces turned in her direction. Shaking and struggling to breathe, Jodie counted them again. *Ten.* Two more than had arrived in the back of the truck. Two more than the coffins she'd wrenched open. *Ten. How is that possible?*

It's a prank. Her eyes danced about the store, skimming over the figures. *It's Earl's doing, I'll bet. He knew I was scared of them; he saw my face when we were unpacking them and the first mannequin fell on me. He was angry because I made him close up himself and because I complained about the alcohol. And he said the mannequins were cheap; he must have been able to buy two more of them and bring them in… when? Tonight? No, I would have heard. It must have been last night. And he destroyed the store while he was here to add atmosphere.*

And then he came back tonight to lock me in…

The mannequins were naked again, Jodie realized. Their clothes lay scattered across the floor. That accounted for the shirt she'd stepped on. The one thing she couldn't understand, though, was why someone would bother undressing all ten dummies… and how she hadn't heard it.

"Very funny, Earl," she called, trying to sound braver than she felt. "Your dad's mad at you, by the way."

Silence. Chills crawled up Jodie's arms, setting the hairs to stand on end. Earl had both the motive and the ability to set up the prank, but the more she thought about it, the less certain she was that he was responsible. It wasn't Earl's style at all. It was too subtle and nuanced—too clever. Earl would have been just as happy to throw a dozen eggs at her car.

He's got to be working with someone, then. A friend? Are they building up to something? Should I get out before I get a metaphorical bucket of pig blood dropped on me?

The store keys were in her bag under the front desk. Jodie skirted the racks to get to it, not daring to take her eyes off the store. There were a dozen places a man could hide in that room without any effort, and being alone in the store while shoppers milled around just outside the windows was very different compared to the isolation once the shops were deserted.

Jodie ducked under the desk to pull her bag out from its shelf. She tugged open the front pouch where she kept her keys and licked at her dry lips as she found it empty.

It's fine. I must have put it in a different pocket; that's all. Everything's okay.

Straightening up, Jodie surveyed the store again. It was still and quiet. And yet, something seemed wrong. *The mannequins.* She could have sworn they'd been facing the shutter door a moment ago, but now they were looking toward the desk. Toward her.

Jodie swallowed thickly as she unzipped her bag and began digging through it. She'd been meaning to clean it out for months—the crumpled receipts, empty tissue packs, mouth fresheners, spare makeup, and hairbrushes hindered her search.

It was hard to focus while she felt so scrutinized. Desperate, Jodie turned the bag upside down, scattering its contents across the desk, and searched for the metallic glint of her key ring. It wasn't there. Jodie swore under her breath. Frustrated, she knelt behind the desk again, running her hand along the shelf in case the keys had fallen out. Nada.

"Damn it, Earl!" Jodie choked as she looked up into the dark glare of one of the mannequins.

It had moved, impossibly, across the store to place itself on the other side of the desk, its hands spread and fingers resting lightly on the wooden surface. The head had turned to the side to regard her, and as Jodie looked up at it, she found there was something terribly, horribly familiar about it.

Earl's heavy brow, his small eyes, his slightly crooked nose, and his thin lips had been warped, changed, and reinterpreted into smooth ceramic and white gloss. The features were simultaneously familiar and hideously alien.

Speechless, Jodie backed away from him, trying and failing to understand what she was seeing. She turned to her left, where another of the mannequins stood beside the shelves of jeans. This one, too, was familiar. Allie's lips. Allie's jawline. Allie's high cheekbones.

"No," Jodie whispered. "No, no, impossible."

There was a crack, and the lights died with a whine. Jodie skidded away from the sound, and her back hit a rack of coats, sending them rocking as the store succumbed to darkness. She turned toward the windows that looked out into the shopping center. Those lights there were gone too.

What is this? A power outage?

Lightning cracked across the sky. The harsh flash burst through the center's skylights and into the store. In that split second, she saw the mannequins had stepped off their stands and come out of their corners to inch closer to her. Earl's mannequin had reached out, its fingers extended toward her face. Then the light faded, and darkness rushed back in to take its place.

Terror made her legs give out, and Jodie tumbled to the ground, panting and shivering, feeling as though she were about to be sick. She could hear them, she realized. Stiff joints creaked as they moved. The faint, sharp taps of ceramic feet on tile accompanied shifting noises as they brushed past the racks, disturbing the clothes.

Think! Think! The store has a generator, doesn't it? Why hasn't it come on yet?

Something cool and hard brushed across Jodie's exposed neck, and she shrank back from it with a gasp. Her skin chilled where it had been touched, as though the ceramic had been frozen. The entire store felt colder than it should have, and her muscles were cramping in the chill.

She couldn't see them, but she could picture them, moving languidly, confidently, knowing she was blind and trapped. The infernal tapping noise was coming closer—so close that they must be on top of her. Jodie shrank down close to the ground and balled her hands into fists, even though she knew her flesh would be useless against rigid ceramic.

A whirring noise shocked her, and she opened her eyes. While the lights in her own shop stayed cold, the main center lights flickered back to life. They couldn't illuminate her store completely, but it was enough, and Jodie risked raising her head.

She was surrounded. Hands extended toward her, faces leaned close, and bodies barred her path. But they'd frozen. *It's the light. They can't move in the light.*

Cold radiated off their ceramic. Jodie shrank as far from the grasping hands as she could, her mind scrambling for an escape. If she could just get outside the store and find a place with lights and other people…

The shutter door was locked, though, and the keys had been stolen. The store windows were reinforced to prevent breaking, and there was no other exit. Except…

Jodie's eyes landed on the door to the storeroom. If she could get through the back room and down the concrete hallways, she would be able to make it to the center court, where the movie theater would still be open. And that meant light and company and safety.

They're slow. She glanced back at the empty faces leering down at her. *Surely I can outrun them.*

The light only penetrated into the first few feet of the store, though. From there to the back room was a mess of shadows.

Go, Jodie urged herself as desperation battled with fear that had frozen her to the ground. *Go, before the lights go out again. Go, go!*

There was no way to push past the mannequins without touching them, so Jodie pulled herself to her feet and threw herself over the top of the service desk, tumbling to the floor on the other side. Her weak legs held her, and she began running between the racks, dodging the clothes on the ground that the mannequins had shed. Her hand latched on to the handle of the stockroom door, and she twisted it, pausing just long enough to glance over her shoulder. The mannequins had turned their heads to watch her progress. Jodie swore as she slipped through the door and pulled it shut behind her.

Apparently, the generator didn't power the back sections of the shops; the storeroom was dark, and there was no sign of light coming from under the door leading to the concrete passageways. Jodie fumbled in her pocket for her phone, but it was empty.

Where...? Of course, on the front desk—with everything else from my bag.

Jodie moved forward, feeling her way along the shelves, until she found the one she knew held the store's branded bags. The quiet squeal of a door being opened sent Jodie's heart into her throat as she felt around the box's base, searching for Allie's phone, and a gasp escaped her as her fingers fixed on the cool metal. She swiped it on, and the weak light spread through the room, illuminating the high-stacked boxes, the layaway bags, the piles of clothes...and the mannequin, standing just behind her.

She backed away from it, keeping her light focused on its face. Its eyes followed her from inside the shadowed hollows below its brow. Jodie reached her spare hand behind herself, feeling for the door that led to the hallways. Grasping the handle, she pulled it open.

The concrete passageway spread to her left and her right. The right path would take her toward the grocery store at one end of the center. The left path led to the loading docks, the center court, and the movie theater. She turned the door's lock before closing it, hoping it might delay the mannequins for at least a moment, then she ran. The motion made it impossible to hold the light steady, and it flashed across the stained concrete floor and dark chipped walls in erratic bursts.

Scraping, dragging, and creaking noises came from behind her. She tried shining the light over her shoulder, hoping that would slow them down, but she nearly tripped in the darkness. Doors on either side of her led into different stores; most of them were locked, she knew, and the ones that weren't locked would lead her back to the quiet parts of the center.

The noises were growing closer, becoming louder, echoing off the concrete and blending with the sound of her slapping feet. She didn't dare stop but sucked breaths into her dry, sticky lungs as stress and exertion caused a stitch in her side. *Not far now. Just the next left—*

A white shape loomed out of the darkness, filling the hallway she'd been aiming for, and Jodie skidded backward, gasping. Her hands shook almost too badly to hold the light on the mannequin that had taken one of the back ways to block her path.

The loading dock! Get outside, into the parking lot. Run for the center court!

Jodie turned, using her momentum to swing herself down the opposite hallway, toward the loading dock, toward the place her nightmare had started. A flash of lightning ahead told her the doors were open—someone must be waiting for a delivery that night—and she raced for them, barely pausing to breathe. A new sound was building and pressing against her eardrums: torrential rain pounded the asphalt as the storm spent itself over the center.

As she leaped into the vast concrete room, another flash of lightning gave her a split-second view of the parking lot. She couldn't see a single car. The rain was coming at a sharp angle, heavy enough to obscure the trees growing by the ends of the parking rows. Litter, leaves, and even small branches that had been stripped off the trees whipped across the asphalt, gripped by terrific winds.

Jodie lowered her head as she dashed under the loading dock doorway. Icy rain stung her face, blinding her, clinging to her hair, and slipping down her neck. It drenched her in no time at all, and she struggled to keep up her speed with the wet clothes flapping around her and a stitch digging into her side.

The center was shaped like a boomerang, with the parking lot nestled against the inside curve, and Jodie could see the lights at the opposite end—with the movie theater and food courts— shining through the rain. Trying to block out the sensation that she wasn't running alone, she focused on the light, blinking furiously as the rain dripped into her eyes and plastered her hair across her face.

She no longer tried to control the light from Allie's phone, but it flashed around her as she pumped her arms. For a split second, the light landed on a ghostly shape running abreast of her.

Jodie gasped and keened right, toward where a barrier of shrubs would divide her from the figure. She turned too sharply and skidded on a patch of oil left on the asphalt. Jodie lost her balance as her legs slipped from under her. Then a white shape appeared out of nowhere, phasing through the rain, arms extended toward her. Unable to stop her momentum, she collided with the hard ceramic and tasted blood. The arms, colder than the rain, colder than ice, slipped around her in a dead man's embrace.

Just like I caught it on that first day.

She struggled to pull back and worm her way free, but the grip was like a vise, crushing the air out of her lungs. Jodie raised her head as thunder pealed above; the deafening noise sent vibrations through her body. The mannequin's ghastly, white face stared down at her, inscrutable in the darkness as rain pinged off its glossy ceramic skin. More shapes were materializing behind it and to either side as the mannequins moved in, surrounding them.

Jodie opened her mouth to scream, and the mannequin pressed a long, frozen finger to her lips as it smiled down at her.

Miho jogged through the shopping center, hands thrust into her jacket pockets as she tried to warm herself. She'd become drenched in the short run from her car to the center's doors. It was terrible weather, and the forecast didn't expect it to clear for another day or two.

Their store's doors were still closed, and Miho allowed her jog to slow to a brisk walk. She was late for the morning shift, but by the look of it, so was Jodie. As she fished her keys out of her bag, Miho vaguely wondered if the other woman had woken up as sore as she had.

The shutter slid up into its case with a scraping, grumbling noise. The inside of the store was intact that morning—thankfully—and Miho had settled into her space behind the counter before she realized Jodie had taken the clothes off the mannequins.

Why on earth?

Jodie clearly didn't like the dummies. After all that pressure she'd placed on Mr. Heinlein to buy them, she'd actually seemed quite paranoid since they'd arrived. *So why'd she go to the trouble of stripping their clothes off?*

Miho began picking the items off the floor and re-dressing the mannequins. If she was being completely honest, she wasn't a huge fan of them either. They were always watching her…which was, of course, impossible; they didn't even have eyes. Miho knew that it was meant to be a sign of good art if a painting's eyes followed someone around the room. She wondered if the same principle applied to statues.

She was slinging a sweater over one of the female mannequins when she sensed Jodie standing behind her. Miho swung around, shocked and half laughing as she said, "Jo, you startled me. I didn't hear you come in—"

The words died on her tongue as she faced the figure behind her. It wasn't Jodie but another mannequin. The face looked remarkably like her friend's, though, almost as if it had been modeled off her. Miho leaned closer, frowning at it, wondering how she hadn't noticed the similarities before.

Then something happened that Miho had no answer or explanation for.

The mannequin blinked.

AUTHOR'S NOTE

Here's a bit of trivia about me: I'm not afraid of clowns.

Here's another bit of trivia: I hate, hate, hate mannequins. It's as though every bit of animosity I should feel toward clowns has been taken and condensed into dread associated with storefront dummies.

This isn't great. In an average day, I encounter approximately zero clowns. But, in an average day at the shops, I encounter significantly more than zero mannequins.

I hate the way they have indents where their eyes and mouths should be. I hate the way their hands are poised. I hate the feeling that, if I turn my back on them, they'll twitch around on their stands to watch me.

Like with all of my deepest fears, I attempt to excise this emotion into my books. I've written two stories about mannequins so far. It has not made me fear them any less. But, perhaps, it will make you fear them a little more.

ABOUT THE AUTHOR

Darcy Coates is the *USA Today* bestselling author of *Hunted*, *The Haunting of Ashburn House*, *Craven Manor*, and more than a dozen other horror and suspense titles. She lives on the Central Coast of Australia with her family, cats, and a garden full of herbs and vegetables. Darcy loves forests, especially old-growth forests where the trees dwarf anyone who steps between them. Wherever she lives, she tries to have a mountain range close by.